the

face

of

a

monster

a

novel

kevin

richard

white

NFB
<<<>>>
Buffalo, NY

author's note

for any young child/teen who has lost a parent

in my case, both. mom when I was nine. dad, when I was twenty five.

The Face of a Monster
A Novel

Kevin Richard White

"Balance is bittersweet when all you know is madness."

- Modern Life Is War, "Dark Water"

"Some part of me knew he would show up, that if I stood in one place long enough he would find me, like you're taught to do when you're lost. But they never taught us what to do if both of you are lost, and you both end up in the same place, waiting."

- Nick Flynn, *Another Bullshit Night In Suck City*

bronwyn

I'm not ready to start the day.

I close my heavy eyes and words form, fill in, fill up my empty.

Endings are elusive, middles are nowhere to be found, but worst of all is to begin, to begin, to begin.

He was right, that man.

I look into the sky that is my ceiling and I see peeling paint and I think of a lot of things I can do to fix the room I sleep in, the room I try to fight my way out of, to go to other rooms. But a lot of what I come up with involves work, and not sleeping, and not lying to people, and forward progress, baby steps. I think of my friends who have moved on, who are no longer here. And I guess when I put it that way, they weren't really friends at all.

Hello, paranoid thoughts. All part of a healthy balanced breakfast.

I sit up in bed and I look out the window, gloomy rain and falling leaves. I check for lumps, all good for another day. I guess I have to look at the bright side. I could be delicious, big-breasted worm food. I could be a bed for some man to lay on top of, to thrust, to give me his goods. God. What a life to live, then, huh? Hey, but that's what makes you famous these days. Just tape it and put it on social media. And then you get followers. And then you get your own series. And then you're gold.

And then you're remembered. Remembered even more than someone who gave to charity, who died fighting a fire, who died writing a book of sonnets.

What am I talking about exactly? Rather, what do I want to be remembered as? Someone who just talks or someone who knows what they're talking about *exactly?* It's a daring decision. Act now, be a hero, forget about the consequences. But I think too much, I know the consequences by names, and so I sit here, looking out into gray, thinking about it all, losing it all, regaining nothing back, and just being so ultimately bored.

I get up. I go to put on the same clothes as before, because that's all we ever are at times. Just piles of dirty clothes. There's smell attached to them, but no one actually sees the work we do in these things. There's rips and tears and strings are loose, but what do they really prove? The workmanship of the person who made it or the person who wore it? I'm thinking too much this morning. I told you I wasn't ready to start the day. I'm not ready to start ANY day. I hate it when I have to wake up and still see dark and fog and leaves, like I can't allow myself one sunrise because it'll cost me too much. Hell, in this town, even the sun is too embarrassed to show its face. I can't say I blame it. Who would want to look at this town willingly?

God. I'm sitting here acting like the weather is to blame for my attitude. No, you got it all wrong. See, I just hate things and people because it's easier and convenient and takes less effort than loving. As I read before on a website, stereotypes are a real time saver. I'm a bitch. I hate anything that even screams capitalism (yet the ironic thing is that yes, I am stuck in retail with no exit) and I refuse to buy into our system that money is success (and yet the ironic thing is that yes, I still live at home scraping by). I hate popular music. I hate Easter dinner. I hate those paranormal freaking a-vampire-loves-a-goddamn-griffin books. I want to live my life in such a way that the Westboro Baptist Church wants to picket my goddamn funeral (take that, you lousy pricks! There, I said it). But I still eschew any sort of activity that implies teamwork and good nature, I refuse to imbibe in pretentious do-goodery unless I know I'm getting something amazing out of it rather than just the fleeting, barely hanging feeling of temporary satisfaction, and I refuse to acknowledge the simple fact that we're just souls meant to have true love and affection. I simply hate things that I think other people love, I love it when the things I hate fail miserably, and I hate the concept of love.

I'm a cuddly little fluffball if you get to know me.

It just boils down to my love, my way. And that love is sharp and not fun. I wind up breaking everything I meet, and that goes for people and things. It just happens that way. Oh, danger and lack of sensibility, you're everywhere I go. Follow me up and down, through and through, and around. And never let me go, you beautiful thing. You're my shield to help me block out the idiots and assholes who don't know right from wrong, and you keep me from jumping into the river at the end of every night with stones in my pockets.

I wouldn't use stones if it came to that point. Dear, I would use bricks.

And leave no trace behind. Yes, sir. The howling wind could look for me for days on end and I would be nowhere to be discovered, laying amongst the grass that's never been seen by man, staring up into the sky, laughing, chuckling, crying with the right words, ready at the helm: "You bastards."

Sigh. I let my imagination get the best of me, sometimes, don't I?

You'll come to see that I'm just more than a person. I'm just a monster, as my father told me once. I think he was joking. But I don't think he was at the same time. I think he was proud that he created someone who was a fighter. But also, he's not around anymore to really see it, having found his death (at the bottom of a bottle) eons ago, so he may not be the best judge of character anymore. Oh, but that insurance policy that we knew nothing about! Me and

Mom are all set for life now, and I just pay my way by standing at register and dreaming about anything that seems better than running receipt tape: being a photographer, drinking a beer, listening to Modern Life Is War, destroying, destroying, destroying anything that even remotely resembles the color pink and/or love.

How could I be so silly? Some people would have another type of name for me, but I've heard it all before, so I won't divulge. There will be time for that all later. You'll see. I'll show you.

Unfortunately I have to open which means I have to inject coffee beans into my bloodstream and smoke a million cigarettes and pretend I'm not dead, so I start the ritual (the toughest one of my life, mind you) of Interacting With Humanity. I put the earbuds in, I turn up *Witness* as loud as I can, and I hear the screams come in loud and clear. I'm allowed to smoke as long as it's in my room (Mom doesn't want to come in here anyway and look at three day old sandwich plates and half-finished beer cans) so I light the hell up and allow myself to get lost in my perfectly assembled city of quotes and floating pictures. And it is a beautiful plain. No sinking ships, no loans, no traffic, NO CUSTOMERS.

I put on those wretched clothes. The Red Button Shirt Of Doom. The bane of my existence. It really goes well with the tongue ring, the nose ring, the eyebrow ring, the red-tip highlights of my hair, my dead eyes, my fangs, oh, Bronwyn, what pretty fangs you have. All the better to show you I'm against you, my dear. (I have to stop calling everybody "my dear", because it just is not true.) The torn jeans, the Chuck Taylors. The bracelets that management told me I couldn't wear but I do anyway (for some reason, they don't want a big black FUCK YOU band on my wrist, I can't see why, it's just a word. All words are harmless. It's the context that YOU put into it that makes it offensive, but after all, they're corporate whores, and I'm just the puppet with the strings). The eyes that they want me to change, but I make them as unfriendly as possible without looking like a slut. Mascara. That's all I need. Because I'm not about to be happy. I'm here to take your money and pretend it's my money going straight into my pocket. If only. When I rule this rock, things will be different. You'll see. I'll go on a hell of a spree and eliminate anything that complains. I have a right to complain. Most people don't. You're lucky you even have money to shop with, you spoiled brat. Daddy's card. Mommy's checkbook. And not a dollar of your own, you inflatable doll with your puffy cheeks and clacking heels. Go out and play in traffic or suck a tailpipe. You don't deserve the riches you think you deserve.

Like I said, I'm cuddly. I'd make a great friend to go mini golfing with. I'd be the one to cheer you along. Maybe we can be friends. I would never do anything to ruin our friendship!

I look in the mirror. I sigh. I'm just restless.

I feel like there is potential in me, like there is a fire that can cover a whole town. But I'm just too tired and too interested in the negative to truly be someone influential or even worth looking up to. Mom tells me I can do things with my life.

And I tell her, "Yeah, Mom. I know." When I clearly don't know what's next. I made mistakes. And now I get to be a slave, and everything else I love, just sits. And everything I hate precedes that now. All the years bring more of the same: hope, crushing defeat, teeth cleanings, resolutions, and something you can't reach because your arms aren't long enough. Either that or that the lies you tell yourself break your bones so bad that you weren't expecting the beautiful pain, and you stay on the ground, staring upwards, because dreams? Shit. They're free. They're untaxed. So take them. Before someone else does.

I stare in the mirror for a long time, watching my new body under these same old clothes. I think of Obamacare. I think of all the notifications that I brush aside. I think of the beer I need to drink. I think of all the wars I need to start and all of the battles I have yet to tidy up with a ribbon. I look over at my Converge poster. I look at all the jewelry I stole that I never wear because it is gaudy and I only took it for the sake of attempting to ruin the system. I look at the moleskin notebook of rants and drawings and poems and manifestos and homemade tattoos that will never see the artificial light of day. I think of creation, what I can do to change how things grow. I smile. I am darkness, a shade unforgivable, a color slightly out of signal with the rest of this paltry multi-rainbow blanketed world. I watch as my mouth matches my thoughts. I WILL BE A PHOTOGRAPHER. I will picture this suicidal place in the right lens. I will capture the apocalypse in an SD card.

My phone beeps suddenly. I look at who it is. It's a reminder for The Church Group after work. I almost scream. I forgot all about it. Mom will flip if I don't attend. A half finished beer sits on my nightstand. I finish it.

It's not even nine.

elaine

I woke up a little unnerved. I couldn't believe the dream I was having.

In it, I was older. I was sitting in a restaurant, waiting for someone to come. I couldn't remember who. But I remember watching the candles flicker on nearby tables. And everyone sitting at those tables looked so happy. They were loving life. Couples held hands, kids played with toys, wine was being poured. It was as if the outside world didn't exist at all, that the only world that was truly alive was in these walls. And I remember not being able to breathe all of a sudden. I choked on air. I choked on water. No one asked me how I was doing. I felt so embarrassed. I excused myself to no one and I ran out, crying. I hurried out into the street and a terrible rain was falling, and everyone still looked so happy even though they were drenched and cold. They were talking in a language I could not understand, and their eyes were so wide, so mischievous, like they had just killed a person they always wanted to kill. I ran to my car and I opened the door and I tried to drive away, but my fingers were going numb. I looked down at myself. I was dressed in a businesswoman's suit. I looked manicured. I looked like I was about forty-five years old. I looked at myself in the rearview mirror and I was aging every second. I vomited into my lap. I got out of the car and I tried to go into a nearby store to clean myself up. And that's where it got even weirder. I walked into the store and the man behind the counter was Dad. And he looked as he did after he got the promotion to CEO. He cut a legendary figure. His blue eyes were on fire. Not a hair out of place. And I said, "Dad, what are you doing here?" I wiped all the vomit I could off my face and I hid it in my pants pocket. And he didn't answer me. In fact, he didn't even say a word - he just poured coffee and watched the TV on the wall and straightened his apron. And I kept saying, "But Dad, you're dead. Don't you get it? Don't you understand? Don't you at least even feel it?" But he felt nothing. He just stood there, like he was tending bar, like he was waiting for soldiers to come in to welcome home from somewhere. I ran to the back of the store into their bathroom and I saw that my hands were trembling so violently that the skin was starting to peel off like an orange. I saw that everything was starting to become orange. And I said, "Dad, Dad, Dad" over and over again and I somehow made it out of the bathroom only to find him standing right outside the door with a cup of coffee in his hand. I was crying and he handed it to me. I dropped it. He merely shrugged and he just came over with a mop to clean it up. And I was hitting him again and again, out of pure frustration, screaming, "Dad! You're dead! What are you doing here?" And he started to bleed and my orange peel fists pounded him and I knocked out his teeth and bruised his perfect face but he just kept mopping and whistling a tune. Finally he stayed down but he was clutching the mop like a hymn book and just smiled. My hands were hanging by a thread of thin bone at the wrist. I couldn't stand anymore. I fell backwards over a display and the jolt -

- the alarm -

- woke me up. I was crying. Mom heard it. She came rushing in.

"Elaine, is everything okay? I heard you talking in your sleep."

I couldn't say anything. I was trying to drink some water. I couldn't breathe or rationalize. I hated being so defenseless, so vulnerable.

"Oh, honey. I heard you say his name." And then her own eyes began to swell with tears, but I wiped them away with a tissue. We both sat there in silence for a while. It was an awful-looking day outside, too. I told her all about the dream and we just held each other afterwards.

"We'll make it through this," she kept telling me, rubbing my back. "We can do this, right?"

I told her we can.

"Yes we will, and don't you ever forget it."

I told her that she was the strongest woman I knew and that would never change for anything. I told her lots of things that involved love and strength, and that even though this was a bad time for us, that things would get better, and I would work as hard as I could to do what's right for this family, given now the circumstances that upended our days.

She smiled at me and brushed some hair out of my face. "You're such a pretty girl. You're going to do fantastic in this world."

I just half-smiled and she left me to collect my thoughts. It's been a tough time lately. It's hard to comprehend with what really happened. I sat up in bed and through my bay window I watched the leaves fall to the ground. I wished I could just sit at home and read today, but there was too much to do. I had to go to work and support group and see some old friends for lunch, but suddenly I didn't even want to leave my room. I didn't want to necessarily go back to bed either, but I just wanted to sit there. But I started thinking about those orange peel hands, and the suit I was wearing, and Dad's coffee cup, so I texted Dylan to take my mind off of it.

He didn't respond right away, but when he did, he said some of the sweetest things I think I ever read. He is such an amazing boyfriend. I wouldn't know what to do without him. Instead of texting him back, I called him and we talked for a while. He didn't even care that I woke him up. All he was concerned about was if I was alright. He really did understand - most people say that when they understand something about you, they really don't. Well, this one, he really does. And I'm lucky and grateful and every word possible. I told him I loved him and he told me to put the past way behind me because I can run faster than it, and that I'll wind up doing awesome things, and those dreams will just be burdens that will soon fade. Like I said, it's love. And it's the best medicine for me, I feel. It is the only thing that can cure a crying heart. Drugs or anything else don't work - they just deaden it until you're caught off guard and they open the door and it all floods back to you. Love will make it all better. That's my ultimate belief. I came to that after I realized those meds that the doctor gave me for my depression made me sick and hallucinate really weird crap. And I realized it was all for money and not for making people better. But anyway. I felt that love while I was talking to him the entire time. He promised he would try to get to see me today, but he was out of town with his family, and he didn't know when he would be back. I told him not to worry and that I loved him so much and I thanked him for everything. I hung up the phone and looked at it for a while, scrolling through the pictures, reading the texts again as if they were new. After I committed them to memory, I put the phone down and I started to get dressed.

Dad's been dead for five months. Needless to say, when it happened, we were all extremely devastated. He was hit by a drunk driver on his way home from work - Mom knows all of the details because she had to, she was the wife and the lover, and she needed to know everything that happened in his last moments because she needed them to complete her life, her last moments, whenever she got to them. I thought that was extremely noble and terrifying at the same time. She knew how bloody he was, what his skin looked like, how sunken his eyes were, even down to the watch he was wearing. But I refuse to know. I don't want to know what he looked like or what happened. It was a car accident - that's all I know. I don't want to anything about his last words because I want his last words to me to be what I remember about him. I called him an hour before he came home to ask him a question about something. I don't even remember what it was, it was so unimportant, but after he answered, all he said was, "Elaine, I love you, and I'm proud of you." That was it. And then I said bye and I hung up the phone. That's what I want to remember. I don't know what to know what road it was on or what the car looked like. Mom knows all of that now, and I meant it when I said she was the strongest person I know because she knows all about death, and I don't want to know anything about death. Not a thing. People talk about light and tunnels and deathbed confession and none of that interests me. In fact, it scares me.

Another reason I don't want to know anything about what happened is because I got into a terrible argument with my pastor about it afterwards. Three weeks after his car accident, they held a sermon in his name. And it bothered me. Because the sermon was not about Dad. It was a regular Catholic sermon that just so happened to have his name mentioned in the beginning. Mom and my grandparents and my cousins were all bawling and praying and asking for forgiveness and I couldn't figure out why. And afterwards my Mom screamed at me in the car on the way home, calling me a bunch of names and saying I was being a horrible daughter for not crying for him in church. Of course she didn't count the three previous weeks that I cried at home and at the funeral, and I wanted to tell her what I was feeling but I didn't have the courage to say even a whisper. So the next day I went to talk to the pastor about it, and he gave me the standard Catholic argument to all of it - God's will. It was His decision and we just have to accept what the Lord does for us, even though it seems skewed and weird to us. And that I need to ask for forgiveness, just like the rest of my family. And I admit this was not my best moment, but I asked the pastor, "what fucking forgiveness? I did nothing WRONG." And then I left. But as time wore on it brought Mom and I together, and we're doing the best we can. It just sucks. The love that I thought I would have all my life, it's disappeared so quickly. And I don't know how and when I'll get it back.

I stop dressing to look at myself in the mirror. I don't see how Mom can say I'm pretty. I think I'm barely ordinary, both inside and out. And I'm scarred. But there's hope. There's light somewhere. It'll take a while.

bronwyn

The day's highlights are few and far between. And it all starts off with the obnoxious twit that I work with. Ok. So I get to work (I can't tell you the name of my store, I don't want you to know where I work, and quite frankly, once you see me there, you won't want to come anyway) and it's me and the Assistant Assistant manager who thinks he's God's Holy Gift to retail workers because he's a keyholder. Which trust me, it's no big deal. So I get there and walk in and he's counting the tills and he takes one look at me and he says, "Are you okay, Bronwyn?"

"What?"

He takes a step back like I punched him because I didn't say it very calmly. Either he's going to get me for my beer breath, my jeans, or something about my soul because it's not like I exactly radiate perfection and/or a pleasant shopping experience. I dump my bag down on the counter and I clock in.

"You just seemed like you were upset about something, is all," he says, kinda backtracking, because he knows he's playing a game where he won't win, because I stole all his pieces.

"Stan," I tell him as I pull things out of my bag (cigarettes, energy drink, a notebook that management definitely does not want to know the contents of), "I'm upset about Somalia. And I'm kinda really upset about the Miami Heat. And I'm really, really upset about Elijah Wood ruining *Everything Is Illuminated*. It's a sore subject. So can we not like, talk about any of this, or in fact, anything that even remotely constitutes conversation or communication?"

He blinks at me. He's holding wads of money in his hand. He looks so stupid. And heartbroken in a way, which for a nanosecond is adorable, but then I remember I could dine on his liver if I really wanted to (NOT LITERALLY) and I soften up a bit. Which is weird for me, because then I have to feel emotion, and remember that thing I said about Interacting With Humanity? Trying not to do it.

"It's ok, though, Stan. I'll be fine. Don't worry. We can talk about work."

The color returns to his face. "Okay. Wow. Sorry, I guess I'm just a little on edge this morning is all." And then he proceeds to ramble on about some sad story that really isn't sad, and I pretend to straighten things, and I'm thinking the entire time, only six hours. Six hours left. That's all I have until I get out of here. I can do this.

But for any of you hapless souls who have worked in retail, you know that you're the victim of a firing squad from the minute you walk in until the minute you leave. Because people come in and they're going to gun the fuck out of you. You are a walking target. About anything, even things way beyond your control. People come in and they complain to you about gas prices, or the cost of cereal, or why their son won't call them back. And you become their stepping stone, their welcome mat, and they don't care if you have work to do or if you're tired. And if you even suggest to them that they're in the wrong at any point in time, they claw. That's why I stopped chewing my nails - so I can have talons to fight back with. It's never physical. Because the customers know that emotional and mental? Hurts SO MUCH MORE. For instance:

A woman came in and she wanted to return something because she's retarded in that she just buys things just to buy them to make herself feel better and then she sees her bank statement and that she realizes she could be feeding her kids instead of buying dumb shit so she waddles in and dumps it on the counter and Stan is in the back being all important so I gotta deal with it. And I open up the bag and what she's trying to return is just mangled beyond belief. Like she sat on it or tried to rip it apart with her chubby sweaty paws. Regardless, my hands are tied.

"I can't return this."

Her eyes widen like a sorority girl's legs after two Coronas at a frat party. She stumbled on her words. "But... but... you HAVE to."

"I don't HAVE to," I said, taking a swig of my energy drink. "I can't take damaged products."

"But... but..." and she hands me the receipt like it's a burning flame. And there it says, on the back of it, our store warranty - returns accepted in original condition. I said it slow and fast. I wanted to provide sign language but that would have killed my argument. Whoever swears first, or takes too long to retort, loses the fight in retail. Always win the wars, my one friend said. Never the battles, but the wars. So I highlighted it and gave it back to her.

"I'm going to call the Better Business Bureau," she stutters.

"Go ahead, I'm going for a cigarette," I tell her. Good thing Stan wasn't out here to take care of this, he would be all "ma'am, I understand" and be a sympathetic pussy about it. At least I'm downright brutally honest with these fools and halfwits. I would never string them along in a lulling voice about how the consumer is being hurt, etc.

She seems appalled that I did not take her threat seriously. She is staring at me with envy and hatred. Evidently her ruby red lipstick and her off-white pearls were not enough to intimidate me so she shoves the bag back in her purse and she defiantly informs me, "I'm going to call the Attorney General!"

And I laughed. I had to admit, it was the most creative bullshit threat I ever heard.

And THEN she got angry. Then she started calling me a bunch of names. Surprisingly, she didn't swear. She called me "slacker" and "loser" and all of this stuff, and I just waved her off and went outside for my cigarette break. Let Stan deal with her. This is his life. This sure as hell isn't mine. I got plans. They're going to be made one day, but for now, all I can do is just get away from what bothers me, i.e. humanity. That damn humanity. Adam and Eve, they really did fuck up a glorious thing. I bet they didn't even like apples.

I sat on a bench and lit up and let the carcinogens take over my body. It was a glorious feeling to feel my body cells die, one by one, thousand by thousands. You can't take it with you. You can't take anything with you, and who would want to? The point is to go alone, to die alone, to start over and not bring anything from this life with you, because you know why? It would ruin the paradise you thought you were making for yourself. And the problems you have? They're just yesterday's trash. Don't carry it around. Let it go. Don't let people go after your heart. They are just blips without momentum, just like you and me. And I hated to be so angry because it was a beautiful day, I had to admit. I won't tell you what the sky looked like, you don't need to know. It was just a sky. Just like rivers. It's just a river. There's nothing beautiful about a specific day's sky, or a specific river. The fact that it

IS a river or a sky is beautiful enough. People get caught up too much on the details of it that they forget to just look at the fucking thing. Look, there's water. Don't worry about the rocks or the moss or the branches or the fish. Just look at it. And take it all in. Don't worry about the shapes of clouds or the shade of blue. Just look at the sky and think about how microscopic and ultimately useless we would all be. I mean, I don't like to think that my body will be dirt one day. I know it will, though. And that's okay. As long as I get to have my cigarette first. As long as I get to pay my credit card bill off first. As long as I get to have my photo album I can publish somewhere. I take a few deep drags. I look around. Maybe I can take a few pictures now before the day gets worse. Which we all know can happen any time, because we tell people to live their lives any way they want. So they shoot up hospitals. So they kill their babies. So they make love and then talk shit on them later. It's whatever. You can't change how people act. You can only change how you defend yourself when they attack. It's true. Don't deny it.

So I decide to sit in the car for a while and smoke anyway, blaring the radio, hearing anything I can just to block out the thoughts that are starting to come in. I panic all of a sudden. I don't want to go back inside. I don't want to be pushed around by people who judge me, who think they're better than me. I never say that I'm better than anyone else, I just know that I see things differently than most people, and I think that makes me more perceptive but not better. I know that I'm in a case of arrested development and that I need to make severe changes, but I'm not a miracle worker. I start to think of really dumb shit and all of a sudden I need air. So I get out of the car and I try to take deep breaths and I realize that nothing is going to help right now. Maybe except a drink, which I can't do because I can't have so I guess I'm not going to get any better. So I just decide to suck it up and deal with it. I slam the door shut and I go back into work where I get to hear Stan's side of the story on how he dealt with that crazy lady (he told her to call corporate and leave a complaint, which basically translates to her coming back and returning it and getting her money back and she WINS which is stupid and it makes me look like a complete bitch which I normally wouldn't care about but today I do because I'm not winning so why should someone else) and then I remember that The Church Group is later tonight and I have to go. Maybe going will help me. Maybe I'll get to make a friend.

I laugh out loud at that one.

Stan thought I was laughing about something else. "Well, it's not a good policy. Good-hearted people get screwed on it all the time because they don't know."

I just ignore him. There's no point in telling him what I was thinking, because then he would care, and then he would fall in love with me, and then he would fall on top of me like a wet sack of potatoes and try to make love to me, and I don't want to think about that either right now. So I start to have a panic again and I excuse myself to a corner of the store where I can work and not be bothered. I don't want to interact. I just want to be a restless ghost, where I can live without thinking bad words.

elaine

I called off work. I knew I wasn't in the right mood. That dream was stranger than any dream I had of Dad before. After his death, I had some sickening, almost horror-movie like dreams of him. But never violent. I don't know why I would think those things. Why would I ever want to hurt a man that did everything he could for me in his short time on Earth? Dad and I had an amazing relationship. I know the unconscious is a wicked beast to handle, and it's extremely difficult to rule over, but it's too much for me at times. It's almost as if it wants me to be ashamed of even being alive.

I think a lot of it, though, has to do with the fact that I was repressing God. I don't want anyone to think I don't love God. Because I do. But I just don't see how that became the one solid answer to every single tragedy. God this, God that, it's His will, etc. Can you blame something eternal on an daily event? I don't know how people can make that rationalization and then sleep calmly at night, knowing that the holes of logic are far and wide. I've argued with Mom about it tooth and nail, until we were both blue in the mouth. But she has thirty years of faith over me and when someone is that firmly rooted into their devotion, with no way out of it other than belief, death and ascension, there's no winning or convincing. It just becomes a debilitating blindness that makes you suffer. She accepts that Dad is gone. She accepts that it was an accident. She has forgiven the drunk driver, who apparently is still free (I don't know what kind of sentencing or punishment he received, but again, my refusal to know all the exact details kills my knowledge of the whole event). She has accepted God's decision to tear the family in pieces. And truthfully I don't buy any of that. Forgiveness does not make the world better. It makes the world worse. Peace and love does not mean people learn from their mistakes. In fact, it gives them incentive to do it again. *As long as people forgive me, I can do this again, because they'll forgive me again. I can commit any sin I want. And I will never learn a thing.* I feel like that's what people do when they do something terrible. I'm not saying all people. Just some. And I love God despite this but I don't think He should be involved in this. Because it's not about just Him.

This is about a father killed in his prime. He worked hard to support us. He was honest, he was hilarious. He did not drink, smoke, cheat or lie. He did nothing sinful (okay, that I know of), he honored all of his commitments, he meant every word he said and never sought out to insult anyone. He was just a man who meant extremely well and wanted to take beautiful advantage of this life he was given. And I think it happened just because it happened. That doesn't mean I'm not over it. It's going to take years to get over it. I'm just at that point where I don't know who or what to blame. I'm at the point where I want to blame God, alcohol, car manufacturers, anything I can just so I know it wasn't me. Because I don't want to be blamed for it. I'm just so mad at times I shut down and I cannot move. Because I relive our times in my head, and when I do, they're so damn dark, struggling to appear in the thinnest spots of light and make themselves clear.

A fog settles in when I think of when we played, when we danced in the living room to old records, whenever I was sick and he would stay at home from work and take care of me. I see his mouth open and even though I know what he says I cannot hear the words. And I try to hear but everything prevents me from leaning forward. It's almost like my brain, again, does not want Dad there at all. And he goes, for a while, to fade off into that fog. And I'm left behind. That's what my life has become. Day by day, I get left behind, and it's always someone else's decision. It's horrible to know that you can't control that. People do these things to you. It's never yourself.

I wanted to call the boyfriend again but I didn't. I knew he was busy. I didn't want to be one of those people who clung twenty four hours a day to them, and I always feared of being that person. The truth is, I just didn't know who else to talk to. Mom already went to work and if I were to call her, she'd think my arm fell off and she would rush home and it would be a conversation I would never leave. So I texted the boyfriend anyway, a big long thing saying I was sorry, knowing he would tell me that I was just being silly and not to worry, but I did it anyway. After I sent it, I just lay back in bed, counting the things in my room. I needed something productive to do until support group. I couldn't just lay here like a lump. Mom would want me to take advantage of the day like Dad would. So I called my friends that I was meeting for lunch, and instead invited them over to hang out. And they did. We sat in the back porch and drank tea and knit and listened to music while they let me talk about whatever. I can tell them things that I can't say at support group. It's weird. I tell different people different things. The sky cleared up a little bit, which brightened my mood. I believe in the small things. The big things, apparently, not so much. But as long as you believe in something, that should be enough.

One of my friends, though, asked me something that I hadn't thought about much. What am I going to do with my life now with knowing that it's

41

not perfectly built anymore? I asked what she meant. And she said that when people are born they have a structure built around them to protect them from the dangers and the insecurities of the world. A mother, a father, a home. And as you grow, get older, learn the alphabet, learn how to walk and talk and hide, you become enamored with this idea that you will always be safe from anything, because that's what you were born with and that's how it was built. And as time just keeps going, you think that nothing can hurt you because it's such a perfect structure. And maybe it gets a little weaker as you get older, but as you do, you become a little stronger on your own, so when the structure finally collapses, you have your own, and you don't need the old one anymore. But in some tragic cases, such as mine, my father's death had weakened that safety considerably, and how would I be able to continue knowing that I would not be completely safe? I just looked at her and said nothing. I tried even a whisper but nothing came out so I just sipped the tea and changed the music. But now that they've been gone for a little while, I can answer it.

I've been on my own before, and I recently moved home, because I just needed time to think about where my life was going. And I didn't think one minute about doing it for safety or that I was born in some type of cage. I believe life is freedom, and if you think that your freedom can be penned up in some sort of man-made or even mentally-made structure, I think that's holding you back from your true potential as a human being. Because when you have death happen to some piece of you, like your family, I think you've seen everything. It cuts you, and it makes you step back, but it reminds you of your freedom, it reminds you about your life, and not at all about what kind of structure you were born in. I wanted to tell her that I didn't believe a word of it. I wanted to tell her that in the dreams I had, I've seen things that I don't even want to repeat to them, because they're innocent people and I'm tainted. I've seen the end of the road, and it was me. I was just recently beating him to death when he was already dead. I'm sure that says a lot about me, but the last thing I'm concerned about is my own safety. I'm not going to let the thought of bars and bolts and nuts hold me back from finding out who I am. I am still so young, and evidently, according to people, very pretty. I'm told that I will find an amazing job and an amazing man (which I guess already has happened, and I hope it's for the long run) and a comfortable house, and it will happen because I deserve it. And none of that has to do with living in some kind of fantasy story. I think she was just trying to make me feel better, but it didn't work. It just made me think more.

I feel like I'm too complex for anyone to understand me fully. I know I'm not a perfect woman. I've moved back into home during the middle of college even though I could go out and have my own place tomorrow. I say what I feel will make other people feel better instead of what will make me feel better. I've been to three different therapists since Dad died, and I lied to all of them, and all of them gave me different medications and different analyzing and different this and that and not one of them thinks that I'm doing anything healthy for myself. Okay, so maybe I twist some words around and I'm mad at God. But I'm never going to do harm to myself or anyone else, and I think that should be where it all ends. As long as I don't do anything to anyone else. I never want to hurt anyone. I just want to love and to be loved. And get over Dad, which I know will happen one day. It just sucks because I liked the life that I had, and he will not get to see what I do from this point on. I know people say, "Oh, honey, angels are always watching over you, he sees everything you do every day" and I want to say, "he's not an angel. He's a person." But that won't win over any hearts. It'll just make people look at me weird. But I can't control what they do. I can only control what they do. Maybe their structure is weakening and they don't know how to stop it. Maybe they ought to take a page out of my book if they want to learn something new.

So I spent the rest of my day cleaning my room. I found some old school things and I looked over all of them, remembering that Dad was there for all of them, and suddenly the thought fired itself into my brain and lodged there: that every new memory from now on would have to be without him, and to create all of those experiences brand new, would take so much effort and power. I'd have to remind myself: Elaine, he's not there. Fuck.

I called the boyfriend again.

bronwyn

I know I can be harsh, and it is intentional, but it's not meant to make anyone run away from me. I have that effect on people. They take one look at me and they have nothing to do with me. It's easy, because then I don't have to do anything. But at the same time, I do have morals, as twisted as they are. I fucking hate a lot of dumb shit, but I know that the world can be beautiful, but only when it wants to be, and I lack the patience or the drive to constantly look for it. That's why I want to take pictures. So I can find it when it's there, and keep it when it's gone.

After I left work, I started thinking more about what Stan said about "good-natured people". And I think that's bullshit. I don't think most people are good-natured all of the time, it's only when they want to be or when something they want is involved. I think people put on a fake happy face and then when people see through it, they get pissed off, and the real side comes out, and that's ALL LIFE IS - when humanity's masks slip, and they pull out their guns and ammo, and they just start shooting. Sometimes literally but always figuratively, they go on the rampage until they get what they want and don't care who they step on in the process. The funny thing is that we are all insects in the end, cosmic specks of crap, and we're going to lose. People act like they can beat death, or outlive it, or cheat it or dodge it or snap it in two or whatever, and those people are so silly. They act like it's a bad thing. I don't know. I'm in a weird mood today. And I'm just spewing out whatever comes in my head. I guess it's better than keeping it in.

So after I deal with that pain in the ass, I think of the other pain in the ass. I think about The Church Group and I get mad. But at the same time, I get the feeling that this will be the night that I finally open up my heart and vomit. Let me explain. Because I've been thinking about it all day now and I guess the only way to just kill it is to speak it. Or write it. Or shout it. Or whatever the fuck you want to call it.

My dad was a prick. He really was. He was a liar and he was a drinker and he acted like he was a gigantic war hero with bugles and swords, but in all honesty, he was in the Reserves, he had a bum leg, never saw a minute of action, and read *Muzzleloader* like it was his second job, and told everyone he could that he went over during the Gulf War and tore shit up, and everyone acted like it was truth (but hopefully everyone saw it as a load of crap) and then when the Iraq War came, he wanted to enlist, but doctors took one look at him and saw that his face was barely hanging onto his skull, and that his liver was puckered and blue and shriveled like a raisin, and mistook him for a homeless man. But he wanted to serve his country, he said, pounding his fist on the counter. But everyone ignored him. Every single person. And I'm glad they did it, because then he would have just went over and got his ass shot, come back in a pine box looking like Swiss cheese. But then I'm glad he didn't because he gave us some moments in life to hate, and that was him staying permanently at home in his recliner and watching porn (when Mom wasn't home, which was quite often) and drank himself literally to death. And I watched. And I tried to stop him for a while. Don't think for a minute that I didn't try to save that idiot's life. I hid the bottles. I watered down the whiskey. I put them under lock and key. But he always found a way. He lost his job. He drove around aimlessly until he fell asleep at the wheel. He did something horrible which I won't even get into, but just let it be known that he was one of the worst people on Earth and no creed or document will ever change that fact. He would lay on the living room floor and talk a lot. He called me a whore. He said I open my legs to anyone who opens their eyes looking for open legs. He called Mom a stupid slut. I kicked him in the head once. He bled all over the rug and begged me to do it again. I picked him up and laid him in bed, and he rolled off, and he found a loaded gun from his past previous unglory days, and he made some dumb threats, and then he went and fired it but he shot the mattress. And that bullet is still in the goddamn mattress, a mark of idiocy in a life otherwise unmemorable. And I stood there, wishing death. Come on, baby, please. Come for him. Just take him down and tackle him and close his throat and burn his skin. And it finally did. It got him. And he laid in the hospital bed and he pointed and he was suffering and took one look at my clothes and my eyes and called me a bitch. And I punched him in the face and he spat blood and the nurse led me out and he died.

The fucking bastard. I can't believe they met a man like him go for so long. He could have hurt us. He could have killed us. And all he left was a stain, a blotch, a smudge, a goddamn spot that just can't get cleaned out. And I want nothing more than the walls of his story to break, to disappear. I am so tired of talking about him. I am so tired of seeing him behind my eyes when I drink, when I take pictures, when I do ANYTHING that involves breathing.

And I'm crying now as I relive that entire episode, and I realize that I just said more there than I ever have in front of that band of weepies. Goddamn it. I hate feeling this way. Like a human. And since I'm sitting in the car, at a red light, I start screaming. At the top of my nicotine-soaked, cancer-infected lungs. I feel blood. I feel a red light zoning in on my head and I want it to stay there until someone pulls the trigger. I feel like a politician who just lost his cozy paycheck and his vacation home. I feel like Metallica when they lost to Jethro Tull. I feel like Holden when he left Pencey. I'm a million different things and I have no home and I want to just die just die already like him not to meet him but to just be around him to know that it's all nothing it's all bullshit it's a car crash and there's no breaks there's no brakes. God. I scream until someone honks the horn because the light is green and I flip off the car behind me and I drive and I hope that there's a monolith or a guardrail or a cop I can collide into so I don't have to go to The Church Group. And there the panic stops. I pull over to catch my breath and I go into a parking lot and I take deep breaths and I remember there's people worse off than me. Bronwyn, there are people worse off than YOU. You're not a princess. In fact, you're barely a smear. All you are, you're just BONES. Don't get so excited. You're just skin that won't be anything anymore than just dust. You're nothing. Bronwyn, babe, you're nothing, and you might as well like it.

The sky starts to bloom into an amazing beautiful dark and despite the silence of this lousy town, I hear an incredible music that covers over the dimness quite well. And there's a sunset that doesn't know what color it wants to be and suddenly I forget about Dad, the bastard. I look at the clouds and pretend they're other things like an idiot. I really wanted to appear as a lighthearted individual in the beginning, but I see that sobriety and angelic qualities are a moot point, now. There's no sense in being something I'm not. We're not our own people, you know, in the end. We're the products of our parents. And I know that Dad is in me, in a lot of ways. Maybe the way I want to rebel. Maybe how hard I rebel, how many times I try to walk crooked instead of fly straight. But do I want to be like that? Goddamnit. What do I even want?

I hit my head as hard as I can against the roof of the car. I draw blood. I smile. I do it again. I try to break my skull on the cheap roof of this Escort. It's all I ever want, sometimes. I'm looking into the falling sun and I smile. All I can do is smile. I know I fucked up my life, okay? Don't judge, don't hate. Don't be jealous. Just watch me as I continue to make mistakes like it's my livelihood. I have one, it's just not here. I reach back into the car for my camera. I take a selfie (I hate the term, but that's what it's called, so live with it) and the blood is visible and there and I remember not to change it later. I take a break to light a smoke and I text my Mom to tell her that yes I am going to By God All That Is Holy

Church Group even though I don't want to and she texts back right away to tell me the usual: honey, I am so proud of you and dinner's in the fridge. Alright, packaged rice and discount pork chops and tap water. Man, I am stoked. Color me excited.

I'm watching cars go by and I can't help but think that I am so much more in tune with the bullshit of the universe than other people. I would never do half the things these people do, but then right as I think that, I can't be like that because everyone has their way of coping with the bullshit. I wouldn't go to Coach and spend a thousand dollars on gloves and shitty handbags, but other people WOULD. And I wouldn't do that, I would go and I would bang my head against the wall and snap my fingers in two and try to say that I was doing it for a good cause and it would be perfectly acceptable because it's the SAME THING. I need to stop being so angry about everything. But that's kind of hard to do because it's so easy. I mean, I was left behind by the man who created me. Who wouldn't be angry? Who wouldn't want to fucking destroy? Who wouldn't want to tear apart the chances they were given when the person who was meant to love you turns your back on you? I look around some more. I want to die and I want to live so I can teach and show people. It's so conflicting. I can't ever decide. There's heaven and there's hell. I can't determine which one sounds better. Hell is for heroes. And Heaven? Who knows what Heaven is for. We'll never know.

I get back into the car. I don't clean up the blood. I let it run and drip. I'll take care of it.

Eventually.

elaine

There's a certain kind of love that I want to be able to teach one day. Once I go and get my degree and my student teaching and everything that they say/think that I need, I want to be able to show everyone what kind of power their mind can have, should they give it the right permission. After they break their barriers down, I want them to see that there is a deep hidden type of love there, hiding, waiting in the dark. And I'm not sure it's unconditional, because that's what everyone goes after, I think. I want it to not even have a describing word, a prefix, a definition, I want something that language won't even cover. And I want it to be a great thing and I want my name to be attached to it so that everyone knows that I did something important with my life. Because I'm tired of Mom always saying I'm pretty. I want to be more than that. And that's why I want to show people that there is love inside of them. But my family will never understand that desire because it's their job to placate. So I have to go to other people. And most of the time, I can connect with them better. Sometimes you can't tell family anything because they sit there and say, "I know I know" when they really don't but they say they do because they think they understand you because they're blood and even if you're blood that doesn't mean you feel the same things. You just bleed the same color.

After I got off the phone with my boyfriend again (who assured me that I was fine and that I was being ridiculous and that he loved me and that he couldn't wait to see me soon), I went into my parent's room. Mom insists on keeping everything of Dad's even though he's not coming back for it which seems normal to me, because she's in a stage of grief yet that a small part of her believes honestly that he'll just walk through the door like nothing ever happened.

It's weird for her. But I don't know what she's really going through, because she created life with him, she bought a house with him, and all I have are memories where he gave me his time. It's odd the way I'm putting things, but that's just how I think. But anyway, I went into her room, which I never do, just because when I was a kid we never did. It was THEIR room. I had respect.

I walked to the closet and all his suits were still there. I looked at his bureau and there was a watch, a fountain pen, spare change, golf balls, a picture of him and a Phillies ballplayer I can never remember. A calendar on the wall, marking important things for work. A hardcover non-fiction about submarines on his nightstand. A picture of Mom and him on their honeymoon. A picture of me. All these things coalescing into one great big fire, one big pit of love and darkness and light. It's beautiful, really, how depressing death can be, when you tally up all the things you acquired over your very short years and you can't take them with you, no matter how small they are. Sometimes words or a dream just isn't enough. You want to go into paradise with full hands and arms. And all you have are wings, even if you get them. Maybe he was lucky. Maybe he got them. I just look around for a while. Mom's side of the bed is ratty, unmade. His side is perfect, in line, a victim of good behavior. I sigh. She can't live like this forever, but it is not my place to ever say. I'm just the daughter. I wasn't the wife. And maybe that's for the best. She can't move on, but she knows I will, and that's why she wants me to keep going to support group, to talk, to make friends. Because she knows that my life can start over. Hers cannot. A kiss will never feel the same, sex will never feel the same, even a dinner date will be hell on Earth. And it's understandable. It's just really sad to me. I want Mom to be better. And maybe I'm in her way. I feel guilty sometimes because since I still live at home, she cannot be free. But every therapist I had has assured me - don't feel that way. You both need each other. And they are completely right and wrong at the same time.

I shut the light off and I go downstairs because support group will start soon. I make it seem like it's this complete world where people go and all of their problems are answered and their sins are absolved. But it's not true. It IS a good place to go, but I feel like my time there is almost over. I can't make friends there. Everyone who goes there complains about their own situation (including me, I know this) and after they all cry, they all go home because they are too tired to do anything else that involves positives. And when I go up to them afterwards, ready to talk, they shrug me off and they pat me condescendingly on the shoulder and just say, "Elaine, you're so brave." But, I want to say, WE'RE ALL SO BRAVE. Don't you see? The anger just kills me. I want to shake them alive, but they want to stay in the realm of the dead. Just because your parent is dead doesn't mean you have to be dead, too. Goddamn it, I want to scream. But I don't. Because it's church. And I shut my mouth. I just say the usual. But today I feel different. I feel like I'm going to say something meaningful today.

I won't talk about alcohol or car accidents or Mom. I'm going to talk about love and creation. And they have no choice but to listen because that's my right to say whatever I want. And they just have to live it because we're all in the same boat, aren't we? We have to learn to co-exist. We're humans. We're not gods. We don't rise above things. We just live and cope with them because that's all we're hardwired to do. We're really not meant to do amazing things sometimes. We're meant to be pathetic and fearful. I accept it at times, but I don't want to be that forever. I want to be above the clouds at least once in my life.

I gather all my things and I brew a quick to-go mug of coffee even though it's close to nighttime. I get in the car and I take a deep breath and I just take a minute to think about things again, which always isn't the best idea. I associate cars with death. I think it's natural, given the circumstances. But I always stop myself and say, *but it's not my death. and it won't be my death.* That's the thought that helps me put the key in the ignition and go. So I do and I just drive. I blare the radio as loud as I can just to block it out. I don't want to lose it on the way there. I want to lose it there. So maybe someone sees how serious I am about changing my life and how I want others to be a part of it.

Maybe I shouldn't talk so much either.

But I struggle so much. I want to be heard and I want to listen.

But I do none of that on the way over. I just drive and then finally I get there. It's at the church where I had the disagreement with the pastor. He's never there but he knows I come to this and I'm half expecting him to show up one of these times so he can try to say something smart to me but he never does and I think it's because he knows I will win in the end. I don't want to sound smug but when I want to fight, I can fight. That always strikes a nerve in me, though, so from the time to the parking lot until I get into the lobby, I fear, and I think, that this will be when he finally confronts me. But I make it inside and there I'm greeted by people my age and we all do the circle-large hug and chat session. Rob, both parents lost. Darren, Mom. Brad, Mom. Julie, Mom. Lisa, both parents lost. George, who hasn't lost any parents but comes because he's a really good guy. And then there's Chad, who's the leader of the support group, a thirty-something who lost both parents to cancer six months apart, and it changed his life, and God had called him to teach others about death. I can't say much about Chad. He can be a little goofy and I think he drank too much of the punch, but he doesn't make this all about God. He makes it about emotion. Which is half the reason I still come and I totally respect him. He's not out to sermon us to death. He's honestly here to listen and to help heal the pain. He can do anything else he wants because he's got a Masters in biology or something but instead he comes to this place and does nothing else except sit and nod his head. And he sees me and gives me a great big hug and just seeing him cheers me up a bit. He asks why the boyfriend isn't with me (he always wants me to bring him and he wants to meet him) but I tell him he's away and he nods solemnly and then he smiles and says, "Well, Elaine, one day, I will meet this man, because he makes you happy" and before I can come up with a proper response, he's off to hug someone else, and everyone's left staring. I guess not everyone can get a hug.

But it takes me a few seconds to realize that not everyone is staring at me. I'm standing half in the entranceway and Bronwyn comes in behind me and she's bleeding from the forehead. I admit, I don't know her very well. She's been here ever since I started coming and she never says a word and I don't think she ever will. But she dresses like a punk and she looks like she just killed somebody and a few people gasp and Chad goes up to her right away and starts whispering in really hushed, calm tones. He's good at assuring people. She half-smiles at him, eyes all weary, and tells him she'll be fine. She's blotting at her face with a napkin and everyone starts to politely disperse. She looks at me and slightly nods her head in acknowledgement, as in, *oh great, you're still here?* And I awkwardly wave until she fixes her gaze elsewhere and ducks into the bathroom to clean herself up. As I said, she's been here for a long time, ever since I was, and all I know is her name and he dresses in black, presumably to piss a lot of people off. She's trying to fit in somewhere. I look back at Chad, who doesn't know what to do. Finally, he looks at me and just shrugs.

"I'm sure she'll be ok," he tells me. "Come on, let her have her peace. She'll join us when she's ready."

He leads me into the gymnasium type area where everyone is sitting in their assigned seats in a circle. It's quiet.

I think of Bronwyn's blood and suddenly I realize I don't want to talk.

bronwyn

So I know I'm bleeding like a stuck pig when I go into the church and it's sacrilege and sin and rapture and all that Biblical term type stuff but I really can't help it because I was just being a human being and that's all they really want from me in the end anyway, right? So I dab what I can and I grab my stuff and of course when I walk in through the front door, everyone is standing there. The only two I really remember is Chad, who's this dopey Mr. Rogers wannabe (although I really shouldn't say that because he's the leader and he never did anything to me personally) and Elaine (who is this super stuffy chick who I know is harboring some deep resentment in possibly never getting laid in her life) and they're looking at me like I'm a freakshow. So I give them a roll of the eyes and I go into the small bathroom down the hall and I hear them whispering and what not and I'm just not in the mood for this today. Or ever. I don't have any makeup to cover up the cut so I just rip off a wad of paper towels the size of a wasp's nest and put pressure on it for a minute or two as I sit on the toilet and let go of my impurities. I laugh. What a situation to be in.

I didn't know I had my hit my head that hard, so it wasn't like I was coming in here like that on purpose. People make mistakes. A lot of people forget that. We weren't born to be perfect little machines and there's people like Chad who say it's ok that we're not but when we come back week after week not having learned anything or not having been better, he's get mad at us and he wants us to start being more "real". Well, I don't know what that means, because I left my mind reader shirt at home. I just find it hard to go out and be real when all you're doing is forcing yourself not to think about something that of course is going to be on your mind all day, every day, because you're HOME and that's where the majority of your memories are. I don't know. I guess I'm just mad because I created a scene and my goal is to not make scenes because Interacting With Humanity is not high on my list. I finish my business and stink up the joint a little and I turn on the crappy fan and I throw the wad down the john and flush and it doesn't look too awful but these people are just going to have to live with a little blood tonight. I snort because there's always those statues of Jesus hanging from the cross in these kinds of places, and he has fake painted blood on him, but they never get mad about that. But when they see it on someone that they have to talk to personally? Oh, man. Get the torches out. We got a monster on our hands. A real live wire.

I walk down the hall into the big room that they always have this meeting in and they're all in a campfire circle in cheap plastic folding chairs, hands clasped, waiting to share their sins and deep feelings. I still don't know half these people's names but they never make any impression on me anyway. Except for Elaine. Something about her bothers me. She always carried herself as this Roman type person - sits up straight, debonair, like her shit don't stink. Honey, I want to tell her. Your shit stinks. We all do. It's because we're human. You may want to put it off as long as you can, but you're just going to fail. I take a seat and I drop my bag to the floor, making a bit of noise. Everyone shoots this weird awkward look and

I purse my lips and try to mentally prepare myself for the crying and banding together that's about to happen.

"So we're all here," Chad says quietly. "Welcome back, everyone. I hope you all have had a fine week since we last met. I understand there's ups and downs in all of our lives, but that is why we have these meetings, so people can get out what they need to get out. So instead of me talking on all night, I want to hear from some of you that I rarely hear from. I want to see you guys run this meeting tonight. I think you guys can do it. You're all strong, young, healthy kids. I just want to see what's going on in your minds right now. Anyone can start off. I don't care what you say, how you say it, but as long as you say something. I want to hear from everyone tonight. Absolutely everyone." And he shoots me a quick look and I widen my eyes and he turns back to the rest of the group. "I don't want to be like the mean teacher in school who picks you out and forces you and alienates you. So it's open. Anyone can start off." He leans back in his chair to signify the end of the monologue. He's probably upset that he's missing a golf tournament on television right now. He seems like that kind of guy.

I scan the room. No one moves. No one coughs for they are afraid that will mark their turn. I fiddle with my bracelets. I look down at my feet. Someone will volunteer soon. They will see the sign of God and they will go trigger happy with their words. I almost want to tell the story of when I kicked Dad in the head when he was drunk, but that's more of a closing story than an opening story. That's like the end of a fire. Someone else needs to spark it.

"I have something," I hear.

I look up and it's Elaine. Her face seems like she's been battling something all day and she's wrestled with that fear but instead of looking heroic and courageous, she looks kinda stupid and blotchy and red. She makes two fists and she rests them on her knees and she tries not to make eye contact with anyone. She's almost embarrassed that this is now her moment. I guess she expected rainbows and flowers and a parade.

"Elaine," Chad says with relief. "Go ahead. The floor is yours."

She remains sitting. She takes a deep breath and she punches her knees lightly and then she begins her spiel. "I was thinking today about love. And creating life. Not the literal, you know, creating life with someone, but creating a new life. And I want to talk about how hard it is. Or how impossible it is. I think that when you're born, you have a predetermined, already sorted amount of love in you. And when it's gone, it's hard to get back because the people who gave it to you, that's unconditional, it's real. I'm sorry, am I talking too fast? I'm just really nervous. I feel like I'm not making sense. Am I making sense? (People nod and mutter, Chad gestures to continue.) I don't know, like, I was sitting with my friends today, and they were talking about structures and buildings and how when you're a baby, you have one already made for you. Like, your parents make it for you. Not a literal one, but like a mental one, an emotional one. And when one of them dies, you...lose some of that support. And you can always find someone else, have someone else introduced in your life that can fill that void, and it never works because it's like a bandage. It's not like it's real material. Like it isn't real love. It's like fake love. And it's building a whole new life over again, with a new building and new stories and new glass and it's just...weird. I don't know if that's what I want. I miss the love that was already there. The love that I had when Dad was still alive? I know that will never come back and that it went with him to the grave. And it's going to be so fucking hard - oh, Chad, I'm sorry, I didn't mean to say that (Chad solemnly nods and mutters something about forgiveness) - to be able to do that. My thoughts are so jumbled today. I had a dream that I was beating up my Dad. He was working in a store and my hands were peeling off and he handed me a coffee and I just beat him up. And he was still smiling. And I realized why he was smiling. It was because it was love. And I know now why my skin was peeling and it's because it wanted me to stop because I was hurting someone I loved. Is this making sense? (more nods, more muttering) I want it to make sense. Because this is what I've been thinking about all day and I want it to be real to other people now. Like, if I have to start over with someone else in my life pretending to be my Dad, it's going to be so hard and so difficult to be able to remember the life I had with my old Dad. Because that's the memory I want to keep. I don't want anyone else, some stranger, to come in and charade and throw words around that don't mean the same. I don't know (she starts to cry) about anything sometimes. I don't want to have bad dreams. I just want to be able to remember the good dreams. But I know Mom is in the same boat as me and I want to understand what she's feeling but all I can do is just think about how I feel and I feel so selfish (someone hands her a tissue, she takes it, Chad is tearing up himself) and I don't want to because I want to be a good person. Is this making any sense at all? It's love. It's about not creating a new life. I just want the old one back. I want to work on the old one instead of coming up with a new one entirely. Just because that structure is just not the same. Sometimes things just can't be fixed. And I love sitting here and listening to everyone and talking to people and trying to figure out what can be done and HOW to fix things, but I'm starting to think that it may not be worth the effort because it's just not the same. I don't even know what I'm saying, I'm just...(stops to dab her tears) I'm confused. I'm lost, I guess. It's hard to be able to say what I really mean, solely because I never expected anything like this to happen in my life. None of us do. I'm just in a weird mood today. I was killing my Dad in that dream. And I just want him back. I don't want to start over." And she stops to have one more big sob but no one comforts her then. They let her finish her big moment with a flourish.

The room is a deathly quiet. Some people seem deeply affected. Tissues come out. Chad is sitting forward in his chair with his head down and his hands together, trying to come up with the right answer for Elaine. I can tell he's struggling. Everyone else seems to want to jump out of their skin. Finally, Chad speaks with sadness.

"Does anybody have anything to say that?"

I raise my hand.

"Bronwyn," Chad says in surprise.

I look at Elaine who's not looking back and I say, "That's all bullshit."

elaine

The voice startles me out of my stupor. I look up. It's Bronwyn who said that. Her, of all people. Her, who never did anything to me or to anyone else for that matter, except sit there and maybe judge, and now she's finally acting upon that feeling. She's sitting there like she's the queen of some deranged domain, in her black and in her blood and her wise-ass remarks. My anger starts to boil up. And she's sitting there like she's ready to rip me open and take my love. She looks like a predator who came in only for an easy dinner. She looks at me like she's expecting me to lose it. But I need to keep my calm. I have to. The therapist told me I have to.

"What did you say?" I finally say.

"I said that's bullshit," Bronwyn says, no anger, no tremor, just a flat line, like she's a ghost, like she's not even real.

"Bronwyn, we will not use words like that in church," Chad says. "I think we need to reel it back in here a little bit - "

"No, Chad," I say. I'm surprised by my volume. "Let her talk. You wanted us to run this. So let her talk." I don't need to snap at him. But I'm hurt. And she chose the wrong person to deal with. I told you about love, I think. And this is how you treat me. The gloves are going to have to come off now. I want to call the boyfriend because I know he'll calm me down. I just wish he was here. So he could see all this. So he could end this so I wouldn't even have to.

Chad slinks back with a wounded face, but he knows what he said, so he won't interject anymore. He gestures back to Bronwyn. "Just watch the language. This is God's house."

Bronwyn sarcastically nods and looks back at me. It's no one house. It's just a building. Her eyes look like weapons. She's fit to kill for some reason. The blood starts to seep out of her cut on her forehead, but it's almost a scratch of pride. "Elaine, you cannot sit here and seriously tell me that you don't want to move on in your life."

"What's wrong with that?"

"Because that means you're weak. That means you want to give up."

"You don't know me. How do you know I'm not weak? I'm not weak."

"Yes you are."

"No I'm not."

"Saying you're not weak means you are weak. You don't get that?"

"How am I weak?"

"Because you just fucking are." Chad shoots her a look and she holds up a hand to say she's sorry. "But you are. You had a dream and now you don't want to move on with your life. You're just content in your misery. You don't want to admit it, but you are."

"And what do you know? What would you know about anything I talked about? You look like you're half-dead. You look like a druggie."

"Elaine," Chad warns.

"Maybe I am," Bronwyn says. "And maybe I'm the smartest person you'll ever meet. Maybe you are. But at least I'm not weak."

"You have no idea what you're talking about," I say, the temper starting to really boil. I start to shake. I wish I wasn't here.

"Yes I do. My dad is dead, too. That's why we're all here. Because someone died and we don't know how to cope with it so we just make stuff up. All of us are here because we don't know what to do with ourselves so we just make excuses and mistakes and hope people will just accept that instead of help us. Well, I'm here to help. And if they don't want to listen to the harsh truth, that's their cross to bear."

Everyone starts to get real uncomfortable. People start to get up.

"Guys, please sit down, we're all in this together," Chad says, trying like hell to get everyone to stick together, but it's clear that this fight doesn't involve them, it's just me and her and no one wants to take any sides. They're very smart people, but I also feel betrayed. Some Church Group. When the going gets tough, they all run like they're needed elsewhere. And they know they're not. So they all start to leave.

Chad gets up and starts to go gently after them, and it's just me, Bronwyn and George.

"I don't make shit up," I told her.

"Yes you do."

"Everything I told you was true."

"No it wasn't."

"Yes it was."

"Ok, maybe some was true, but not all of it. And you know it."

"I don't know what you're trying to prove, but it's not funny. I try to talk about something that I honestly feel and something that bothers me and you sit there and you talk like it's all bullshit and that's not very - "

"Because it is bullshit," she says quietly.

I start to gather my things up to leave. I'm not dealing with this. George tries to put a hand on my shoulder to calm me down, but I shoot daggers at him and say, "Don't you touch me." He acts like I kicked him the gut. He gets real sad and I want to help him but she does not let me say what I need to say to him.

"How can you lie to yourself like that?" Bronwyn asks me.

I turn back to look at her. George starts to leave as well. I hurt his feelings. He was just trying to be a good Christian and I regret snapping at him too. I just realized that I'm never going to be invited back here again. And that may or may not be a good thing, but I'm in too deep with this argument that I really don't care anymore. I guess some things you just have to do alone. She's looking at me with this dead face and sly grin and I want to punch her like I did to Dad this morning and I start to tear up again because this is not behavior he would not approve of. He would really punish me if he saw me like this. And now I'm betraying him and I just want to crawl away. But I lost all feeling. I'm too numb to even think straight. I can't find the words to respond to her accusation. So I just stand there. She wipes the blood off her forehead and she just lets it on her hand. I'm half expecting her to drink it. She certainly looks like the person who would do it for fun.

"Do you even know the opportunity you're wasting to start over? That is the greatest thing you can do. Are you that blind and dumb to not see that? To start over and be new. And you're too fucking stupid to see that. You can do amazing things, you can start over and not worry about any of this. Do you know how great of a feeling that is, how great of a chance? Are you that blind, Elaine? Are you that stupid? You're going to sit there and worry about some dumb dream you had? My dad's been dead for YEARS. And I changed. I don't let him influence my decisions. I don't let his love - or lack thereof - bring me down. The man was a bastard and he did horrible things. I don't let it get to me. Maybe you should do the same thing. I cannot believe you're too stupid to see that. You have a perfect chance to create a new life and you're too worried about love to move on."

"Just shut up. Just shut up and don't ever talk to me again," I told her. "I don't want anything to do with you. You have nothing to do with me. You don't even know me. And I certainly don't want to keep knowing you."

"I don't have to. I'm just trying to help. No one ever helped me with this."

"Well, you're really bad at it, Bronwyn. It looks like you need help. You come in here with blood on your face. Just leave me alone and don't talk to me again. Go open your legs somewhere." It was a very immature thing to say, but I wanted to go to the heart, and that was the best thing I could come up with. But it worked. Because she got up and she looked like she was ready to go in for the ending, the kill. And I was ready. I started to hear the therapist's words creep in. Don't do it, don't do it. But I was begging at the same time. Just do it. Do it right now. So I'm justified. So I have a reason this time. There's no one around.

I told her as much. That if she was going to swing, she might as well do it now.

I saw her eyes grow dark, just like evil. I was looking into a face that I didn't think was a face anymore. It almost seemed like a story that had no quality or affection or symmetry. A face with flat bones, with loveless ground. She looked like death. And I did too. Because we both have it. We both have seen it. But that doesn't mean I have to like her. It doesn't mean anything. It means that we're just both in our own little world with no way out and even though she seems like she's miserable, she's happy. And I won't abide by that kind of misery. I just won't. I deserve better than all of this. I don't deserve to see this face and have this blood so close to mine. She looks like she was just in a street fight and she's desecrating God and I just want Dad back so I wouldn't have to go through this bullshit.

"Elaine," she finally says.

"What?" I ask her.

And some time passes and I'm still seeing the same loveless face but she doesn't do anything. She just closes her eyes and turns around. And she goes back to her seat and she gathers up her things. I almost feel sorry but I don't. I just can't find it in my heart to forgive her. There's a lot of searching going on in my mind right now but there's no passion, there's no emotion. I just feel like I lost. I feel like I blew my chances at ever understanding things. She stops and wipes her forehead off with her sleeve and she turns around and I see her searching for the same things, but I don't think she feels sadness. I don't know. I know she was trying to help but I wasn't looking for help. I just wanted to talk. She reaches into her bag and pulls out a cigarette and puts in her mouth but doesn't light it because she remembers where she is. I try to find the right words.

"Bronwyn," I begin to tell her, my voice choking.

She reaches into her bag and she pulls out a small camera. And without any warning, she takes a quick photo of me standing there. And then she puts in her bag and she walks away. As she's walking to the exit, Chad walks back in and stops her. I feel rage in his voice. He says something very sharp and nasty to her and she just nods and walks away. I stand there, confused, wondering why she took a picture until Chad walks up to me with the same rage. We're the only two in the room. Except for the ghosts.

"Don't come back next week, please," he tells me. "Take some time off."

And then he leaves me there alone.

bronwyn

Right before Dad died, he came into my room one night. When I was writing in my diary. I know, I'm embarrassed about having a diary, but there are some things that people still do, and that's one of them. It's not like I was writing about what boy I liked or what band I was listening to. Alright, I'll be honest. I was writing some pretty suicidal thoughts, but I only felt like that when Dad was alive. I did want to kill myself, for a short while. But that's a stupid phase that only lasted for a little while. I don't like suicidal people, but then again, we all are on some level. Okay but anywho. I was writing something very personal when he came in. And he was drunk naturally. He was the poster child for failed dreams. He claimed that my birth was my fault because I robbed him of an adulthood. He was only 20 when he had me. Mom was 18. So yeah. He claimed it was all my fault. And he came in reeking of Johnnie Walker. I was used to that by now. But I wasn't used to the threats. Up until then, he was just drunk and stupid. But before he died, he got nasty. And started to become more physical. And I couldn't push away from that. The words, I could. The movements, it was like a dance I couldn't learn because everything was broken. It was hard to move away from that kind of music and step.

Anyway, he saw me writing in my diary and he wanted to know what I was writing about. When I told him it was nothing, he believed it was about him. And it was, in a way, but I threw it to the side and expected a fight. But instead of ripping it out of my hands or hitting me, as he started doing, he suddenly became very sad. He collapsed into a nearby chair and downed the rest of his whiskey. And then he started talking about his brother, who was very successful and didn't associate himself with us because we were "low-class trash". And I didn't know why he was thinking about it, and that isn't the point, but what the point of this was that is that he said to me that he was ready to die. And I started telling him I didn't want him to, even when I did. I wanted him to die so that my life would be easier. But he just kept crying more and more and he said he missed Mom (she went to the beach with her friends that particular weekend) and I actually held him. I held him as tight as I could and he started to vomit whiskey on me but I didn't move. He just kept crying and letting it go and I wound up wearing everything he had in him but I didn't move, I didn't mind, I just let it cover me. Because it was his. It was my father's and I needed to show him respect. And he finally stopped vomiting and he couldn't stop talking about family and blood and how things can't be erased, no matter how bad you fucked up. He was very sick but he was also very right about things, for once. And I let go and I started to take my clothes off to change and he started watching me. I thought nothing of it because he was my father and he had seen it before. It's not like I had issues about that. I just figured it was okay.

And he said to me, as he cleaned his mouth off with his sleeve, "You're beautiful."

And I didn't know what to say. This was a few days after I kicked him in the head after he called me a whore and called Mom a slut and he fired his gun into their mattress. I felt omnipotent for a brief second so I whispered to him, "Is that the same as calling me a whore?"

I knew he wouldn't remember that so he said, "What are you talking about?"

"Nothing," I said as I put on a new shirt.

"Fine," he said as he pulled a new fifth out of his coat pocket and poured himself a new glass. He was always wearing a winter coat then because he was freezing because he was dying. And he threw the cap on my floor and poured himself a drink up to the edge of the dirty glass. Suddenly he saw me watching him. He said, "Have a drink with me."

This was when I didn't start drinking yet. I didn't want to be like him. So I said, "No."

"Why?"

I didn't say anything. I didn't have the strength. I wanted a new life, then, briefly, I remember that, because I saw the puke-stained shirt on my floor, and I thought of all my friends that have perfect families, and then I remembered there is no such thing as a perfect family. There's just tolerance and nothing else. Finally, I said, just to give him an answer, "I just don't feel like it right now. I want to go to bed. I have work in the morning."

He sat for a minute taking that in as I cleaned up my room. There was no sense kicking him out. He would get angry about it so I let him sit until he made up his mind. But then, as I was expecting just silence about him, he finally said in a broken voice, "Please."

I turned to look at him. For once, his face had a softness I hadn't seen since I was a little girl. He looked like he was a strapping young lad again, ready to take on the universe. I've seen pictures of him when he was my age. He looked like a real heartbreaker. I could see why Mom fell for his bullshit. He looked fearless. But then he was missing most of his teeth and his eyes had bags as heavy as bricks and he looked at me until I saw the voids behind his sockets. "I'm so tired of doing this alone."

The words spilled out before I could think of them. "So stop doing it."

He thought for a second. "But what else am I going to do, Bronwyn?"

Stop drinking, I wanted to scream. But I did nothing except stand there watching my dad start to die. He had a terrific Irish brogue. He was a hell of a carpenter, a part of a union and everything. He had great taste in music. He had an infectious sense of humor. He had everything a father should have. Except luck and self-control. He had nothing in him that said, **_stop_**. So he kept going. He was on the fast track since Day One to just curl up in a ball from the cold and give the fuck up. He had no future lined up in his head so he was content with this. I thought it was admirable and retarded at the same time. It was so weird.

"Bronwyn," he said. "Do you know why I named you that?"

I wanted to make him laugh. I remember that clearly. So I said, "Because you had too many friends with daughters named Shannon?"

And he chuckled and then he let loose with happiness. A hearty laugh that shook the whole room. He almost spilled the whiskey. And I laughed too. It was a rare warm moment during those times. So I decided to run with it.

"And you're Irish. And you're drinking Scotch whiskey? Man. Everyone will be so upset when they find out you turned your back." I said it lighthearted and I meant it as a gag. But then all hell broke loose.

His light dropped. He suddenly prepared for a battle of which there was no barriers or shelter. He became a warrior and a demon I became scared of. He was everything I know I couldn't fight against or win. My father had become a person that did not matter in life because his death was coming. So he became the worst thing that I could imagine, at least at that point in time.

"What is that supposed to mean?" He said, snarling. He took a long pull of his drink. That was the cue that something was going to happen.

"I meant nothing by it," I said.

He took another long pull. By then the glass was finished. It was always was, then. By about three drinks, it was gone. I wanted to look for something to defend myself with, which I knew was silly, but was completely practical. I had nothing. So I had to weather the storm as best as I could. He stood up and he swayed. He set the glass down. He was shivering. He looked ready to go right into the family plot. I went to hug him again but he stopped me again.

"What did you mean by that?"

"Nothing, Dad. Fuck."

"I named you Bronwyn," he said, "because I needed you to be strong. And you're not being very strong right now."

"Yes I am." He had no idea how strong I was at that moment. I would have run yelling a year ago. But I was holding my ground.

"You're backing down."

"I don't know what you're going to pull next, Dad."

That stopped him. He swayed some more. He knew he was going to lose the battle so he went to subjects he knew nothing about. And like I said, this was the beginning of the end. He didn't know what he was doing. So he would say anything. I forgive him. I don't blame him. Because this wasn't Dad. This wasn't Michael Declan Sullivan. This was just a man who happened to wear clothes and had terrible thoughts about terrible things.

"How many of those high school boys have you fucked?"

"Dad."

"How many?"

"Dad, stop. You're drunk."

"I didn't raise a daughter just so she could open her legs to every fucking cock that walked past."

"Shut the fuck up."

"What did you say to me?"

"I said, shut the fuck up. You fucking drunk."

He went to hit me but he stopped because he could barely lift his arm to complete the motion. So I made two fists of my own. And he laughed at that.

"What, you think you're a fighter? I didn't raise a fighter."

I couldn't say anything. I thought I could handle him.

"Your mother," he said, "would be so ashamed."

"I think Mother would take my side," I said quietly.

"Who the fuck do you think you're talking to?" He said to me.

"I don't even know," I said through tears. I didn't realize I was crying.

He saw my tears. And then he laughed again. "Good. You're crying. You lose. One day you'll be strong," he said to me, and he came up to me, and walked through my fists and hugged me and he kissed me on the cheek. And then he stumbled out and I punched a hole through my wall and then I smoked a cigarette in the house. Fuck him. It was the last kiss I ever had from him. A week later, he finally wound up in the hospital. He found his way and I became stronger.

I say all this as I sit alone in my room at my desk on the sixth beer of a sixth pack. I'm halfway gone. I want to say I can drink more but I can't. I would have made him proud if I could. I started thinking of Elaine. All of what she said made me relive that for some reason. I needed to apologize to her somehow. She actually showed real fight, honesty and love.

So I called Chad.

elaine

I sat outside the church in my car and I tried to call Mom, but her phone must have been turned off. Straight to voicemail. I didn't want to tell her the whole story through a message, so I just hung up. It would have to be face to face, a conversation I did not want to have. So I wound up driving around for a while, to create the illusion that I was really at support group. I stopped off at the diner and had a cup of coffee, although it tasted horrible and I really didn't want it. But I sat there for a while, looking at people, looking at families, trying to come to grips with the situation that I had just faced. I wound up pouring sugar after sugar into an empty cup, just swirling it around, just creating something, anything, to take my mind off what just happened. I had the feeling everybody was watching me and I couldn't shake it and I started to panic. But eventually I was able to black it all out. I would have that feeling for the rest of my life. I would just have to learn to go into a darkness and imagine other things.

I couldn't believe that there was people like Bronwyn in the world. It just didn't make any sense to me. I did nothing to her. And if she was trying to help, it was the worst possible way in the entire universe to help another human being. You don't curse at them. You don't talk down to them. You have to let them know that they are on your side, not alienate them and make them feel like garbage. It wasn't right. And the whole night, maybe my whole perspective on the concept of support, was ruined. How could she live with herself? Maybe she couldn't, and that was the point she was trying to make. That she was truly utterly alone, and that the first person who crossed her path that talked about trying to become better, that she was going to shoot down and make her own little personal plaything out of the remains. I shook my head. I never want to see her again. And that anger I felt when I was in the church was starting to come back while I was sitting there in the diner. It was an anger that all my life I had that I never wanted to use. But I have on several occasions. And it's made me into someone that I never liked. It was hard to control. I couldn't ever kill it, but I had to keep it on a leash. And that's why I don't think of myself as pretty, like Mom said. I just think of myself as ordinary, dangerous.

I grabbed the coffee mug and put both hands around it. And started to squeeze. And my face started to get red and I really tried to crush the mug in my hands but I couldn't do it. Maybe I am weak. Maybe she was right. I poured all the sugar out of it and wiped it onto the floor. I set it aside and I paid the bill and I got out of there. I had about a half an hour before it was an acceptable time to go home so I decided to go to a place that I hadn't been to in years, not since I was a little kid. Maybe it would help the scars that were forming.

Dad used to take me to this ratty park when I was younger. The slide was rusted, the swings were uncomfortable, I always got splinters, the woodchips hurt like hell when you landed on them, the paint was all chipped, and honestly, it looked like shit. But it was our place. It became our little spot when we both needed to get out of the house. And that was a beautiful thing because we loved it and it was ours. Rarely did we ever see anyone else there. Maybe they saw us first, and decided that they could not impede on our world. Or maybe I was just too selfish with everything. Because I would run back and forth between the slide, the swings. And I would scream and shout and he would have to struggle to keep up with me. To push me there, to spin me here. And he would get very tired and he would have to tell me to slow down. *But, Dad I'm a kid*, I would think. I can never slow down. But eventually I would. And he would sit with me in the grass and tell me what it was like to be an adult.

Now I wish I would have never asked him. Because now I know. And it isn't fun.

I got there and of course not another soul was around. The sign had always said no trespassing, but I guess recently someone crossed it out with a black marker. It's not like it ever meant anything anyway. I walked up to the slide, nothing had changed. So I climbed up the steps and stood on the tiny platform and looked around, like I was on a pirate ship, overlooking the sea. But all I saw was houses and lights and people who lived in them that were not happy. It was a feeling you don't have when you're smaller. You just don't think of burdens like that. I decided to go down the slide, for old times, but I got stuck on it halfway down, and I just laid there in the middle of it, looking up at the stars, thinking of how beautiful they look even though they were dying and out of reach and completely nonsensical. About how they're strangers we will never meet, never touch. Their love for us will never be enough, because even in their dismal distance they give us a show that we always take time to look at. It was almost comfortable enough to go to sleep on. I had nowhere else to go for a little while. I had to worry about my life, at least for an hour. I owed myself that much. I needed to remember to love myself instead of trying to force it on other people. So I watched the stars on the rusted slide of my youth, how they danced, how they tried to come down to Earth to be with us all. Silly Earth. A perfect place, and all of these people who have no idea to live on your land. I started dreaming about language, and poetry, and how it should be above all else, and how no one should ever have to live without it.

Suddenly, my phone rang and I fished it out of my pocket but it was an unknown number. I just let it go. I never pick up on unknown numbers. I just don't trust people now. If it's important, they'll call back. Besides, I didn't need anyone else. Not even the boyfriend. Not right now. He would understand. He's an angel. I can't imagine anyone else like him. I'm so lucky to have him. I know he feels the same way about me. I don't even have to hope. Not about that, anyway. I don't have to hope about everything. Just certain things. Just upon these stars. I laid there for a long time. But I decided to go home. I started looking around at the dirty grass and the woodchips and everything had the ghost of Dad attached to it. I could smell him again and hear his voice and I wasn't prepared for it. I could always come back. He would be here, freezing in the cold, staring at the moon, telling me about how simple love can be if you use it right. I'll never forget the day he told me that.

I drove home, listening to music, trying to find new noise in old lyrics, couldn't come up with anything. Nothing changes.

I walked through the front door and Mom was in the kitchen, baking something, and she was very happy to see me, and I had to admit, I was happy to see her. We hugged for a while and we talked briefly, but she saw how tired I looked, so she whisked me off to bed. I was grateful for that, I guess. I was mentally drained. I went up to my room and climbed into bed and I was going to write the boyfriend an e-mail instead of calling him because I was afraid of falling asleep on him but just when I went to compose one to him, I saw I had one from an address I didn't recognize. Normally, I never open up unknown e-mails (spam! I don't need penis enlargement pills, thank you), but this one is titled simply "Tonight". So I clicked on it. And wished I didn't.

"From: deathwish129@gmail.com
To: elaine.meadows2003@gmail.com
Subject: Tonight

elaine,

ok, so, you think this is creepy, and I know this is creepy, but drastic times call for drastic measures. it's bronwyn. from Church Group. before you freak out and call me stalker extraordinaire and call the fuzz on me, I got your address from Chad. He gave me your number, too. I called but you didn't answer. I don't blame you. I wouldn't answer on me, either. but that's not the point of this. he gave me your contact info because i wanted to apologize. i really do. that wasn't like me, what i did tonight. well, maybe it is sometimes. But I was way too fucking mad about that earlier. i don't know what got into me. i guess i heard you talk so passionately about something i buried so well that i got defensive. like i thought my dad was coming out of the grave to come kill me or something. stupid, i know. really stupid. but look, Elaine. I'm sorry. I am. when i called Chad, i was slurring over my words because i really wanted to stress that i wanted to apologize and make things better. look, i know i look like a mess. i know i dress like a druggie. but i'm not. what i did was after my dad died I found myself. i really went and found the shit of myself. and this is what i am. I bleed and i listen to music and i drink and i work and i take pictures. and that was not meant to creep you out, me taking a picture of you. I'm a photographer. ok, well, i want to be a photographer. ok, anyway, i'm trailing *off the topic. the point is, Elaine, is that tonight you showed more fucking heart and blood than half those clowns there. I mean, Chad. Yeah, that sucks what happened to him but I mean he wears sweater vests, ok? he's never going to leave white fence suburbia. those other kids? yeah, i know their pain. Their pain is real and it sucks but that doesn't mean I have to like them. but when you said what you said tonight, it just got to me. it meant a lot to me. and yeah, i got defensive. i got a little harsh. didn't mean to. you're a good person. you're not weak. if anything, i'm the weak one here. i oughta grow the fuck up maybe. you seem like you got your head on straight. look, all i'm saying is i'm sorry. and yeah we're out of the group now it seems so look. i'm offering you the olive branch. let's make peace. that God fellow would want us to. here's my e-mail. you have my number, still in your history, I trust. Call it. write back. do something. if there is love to be shared, i must learn.*

bronwyn"

bronwyn

The lyrics to one of my favorite songs go as follows: "Still tasting youth's bitter exile here in your empty generation's wasteland/Where all the things that you've been clinging to are being ripped from your hands." I find that there's a remarkable truth and tragedy in that. Whether or not I choose to act upon it - that's the difference between listening to something and accepting it as a song or doing something about and accepting it as a movement. And lately I've been following that philosophy. To get up and do something about it. I'm tired of having things ripped from my hands. I want to take what is mine. I want to fix things. Sometimes I give the air that I want to break things. And yeah, I do. But I break them BECAUSE I want to fix them. My mind can get cloudy like anyone else's, but I want to shake the nasty weather out. Which is why I e-mailed Elaine last night. I actually forgot all about it until I woke up this morning and saw a ring of empty beer bottles around my laptop, the page still up. I reread it with incredibly bleary eyes. And it didn't even sound like me. But I knew it was. I knew it was the person that was hiding in me for a long time. That forgiving, reassuring soul, that people would want to know, if they could get past the clothes, the darkness, the immeasurable amount of hate that I have for a lot of things. It's okay to hate. Don't tell me otherwise. But it's okay to love, too, and that's what I need to learn. I have to start accepting people like Elaine in my life, whether they want to or not.

Maybe I'm losing my carefully crafted edge of bitterness. Maybe it's time I let go of my heavy duty reinforced armor that I use to block the advances of positives and optimism. Maybe it's time I stopped screaming about the elitist power that rules the world and how it uses stuff like Facebook to keep us at our preferred title of "drooling idiots". Maybe I should smile.

I look in the mirror and smile. Ugh. Okay, maybe not.

But I'm caught off guard by my sudden change of attitude. What the hell was it exactly that I was trying to prove with that e-mail? I don't really know. It's hard to find an answer so early in the morning. I open the window up and it's actually a gorgeous day. That will change, too, I know it will. I sit naked on the edge and smoke a cigarette, to hell if anyone can see me. They'll probably call the cops and report me for indecent exposure. Fine by me. We're all naked under our clothes, grow the fuck up, I'm not saying we need to be like Sweden or Switzerland or Amsterdam or wherever it is where they let youths walk around in their birthday suit, but people are way too stuck up these days. It's skin. It's not like I'm walking around with Nazi signs or confederate flags or the lyrics to a Kesha song on my body. Because THAT would be offensive. But bare skin - there's nothing wrong with it. So I look over my neighborhood as I smoke two in a row and I contemplate just what the hell I'm going to do about things. I can't even come up with a proper answer. It almost feels like yesterday was just a really bad, not hilarious dream where all of this weird stuff happened and none of it makes any sense. So I went to work. I bashed my head against the car. I fucking flipped out on someone completely innocent in church. And I got myself drunk and wrote an e-mail to the girl that I flipped out on. And then I went to sleep. It's so strange. I must rectify this strangeness somehow by doing something that I care about, that doesn't involve me feeling like my mind is crawling out of my ears.

Since I don't have work until three, I'm going to take advantage of nature and make it my bitch. So I get dressed in pretty much the same outfit as yesterday (Norma Jean shirt instead of The Red Button Shirt Of Doom, torn jeans), grab my iPod and car keys and smokes and my camera and head out to the woods near my house where no other sane person my age will be because leaves and tree bark bore them. Mom asks me where I'm going. She actually looks like she's in an amazing mood today. I'm happy for her, so I decide I'm going to mess with her instead of telling her the truth. I tell her I'm out to go find Jimmy Hoffa. She just smiles and waves me off. Fine by me. It's better to do this kind of stuff alone. No one understands. They don't have to. It's my life, not theirs.

I get to an abandoned spot in the woods and I park my car right next to a tree stump and I step out and there's leaves and branches and water everywhere. It's the perfect area to get lost in, to forget all about drunk fathers and harsh words. But even when I try to get as far away as I can from him, he lingers, he stays. The smell of him, the memory of him is enough to make me sick sometimes. But I shake my head and light a cigarette and walk down the rough dirt paths to where I know there is a river that I love. It's almost like a second home, as secure as a stone basement where no one can get inside, where no human other than me can find solace. I have never shown it to anyone, I have never seen anyone else there. I hear the birds calling and the wind whistling and it's almost like I'm a completely new person because years ago I would have never imagined finding myself here. I was too busy spending time in hospitals and clinics, holding my dad's trembling hand, staring into his beady shitty eyes and telling him it will all be okay, loaning him money I never got back, trying to decipher the lies he was telling and trying to translate it back into truth for Mom and all of us. I would fail. He's right. I did fail a lot. But he failed the most out of us, because he isn't supporting us, because he's gone, because he

106

failed to look into the sky and call it a sky. He just looked at the world and shrugged his shoulders. Fuck him, then. Fuck people like him. I finish the cigarette and I put it in my back pocket. I may be a horrible person, but I won't ever litter. That's just being a douchebag.

A panic attack starts to creep in here of all places but I just light another cigarette to combat it. I'd put music on but I want to hear the sounds of nothing around for a while. There's a golden quality to this silence that cannot be matched. Towns and cities, suburbs and white picket fence hellholes, they'll never match up to just this. Leaves dancing, a branch breaking every now and then, sunlight just pouring in through every available hole and gap down to the cold ground. It's where I would want to live if I had the choice and the money and the motivation. Maybe someday. I keep walking until I hear the river. I know it hears me because it is calling me loud and clear. It's been waiting for me to come by. I walk over huge stones and fallen trees and I climb over a small hill that has been tagged with graffiti and I curse at the ignorant assholes who did it (in my head) and I get to where I want to be. And there it lays, crossing and cutting into the ground, marking its territory like a king. The beautiful thing about some place like this is that it will never alter its course. It will never rewrite its story and I will capture it in a picture to make sure it never does, that it never lies to itself.

I get to water's edge and I take off my shoes and socks and I dip and then submerge my feet into it. I finish smoking the second cigarette and put it in my back pocket. I look for the best shot to start taking pictures but instead I put everything aside and lean back and allow myself to lean into the mud and I just start thinking. I manage to push work and failure out of my head and allow myself solely to concentrate on the benefits of being alone. There's nothing here but an air that knows nothing about death, trees as towers, everything else fitting nicely into a puzzle that managed to find the right form. It just keeps going, cycling. It's a fiction that is true, a film that will not run out of reels or actors. It's a work of God, although I don't believe in Him. I know that contradicts itself, but everything about me cancels itself out. I'm fractured. Some people have to be. Otherwise we wouldn't know what balance is and how we can attain it. But as far as the God thing, I can't put all my faith into something that supposedly can make all this and still let people destroy it. If that were me, I'd kick the shit out of anyone who tried to set fire to all this. It's just not right. But I guess that's why I won't be a part of the Bible anytime soon. I have too many errant thoughts that involve degrading a religious figure. I mean, I can put blind faith into a chair, because I know it's a chair. But something like Him? Sorry, can't do it. I mean, I appreciate it and all, but...you have enough followers. It won't make a difference if I don't follow. It's not like this is Facebook or anything. You have plenty of likes.

I laugh like a fucking maniac at that and I don't know why. I'm happy. I settle back in the mud and I light another cigarette and I close my eyes and I hear my Dad's voice all of a sudden, like a bomb that finally was set to go off at this time.

I remember when I first told him I wanted to look into photography. His response? I barely finished high school. What makes me think I could do something as serious as that? He said the job I have, I might as well stick with it because that's all I know and I won't be able to do anything else. So that was that. And me thinking about it now almost just killed my good mood. But I won't let it. And see, you will never be able to block that out entirely. Even when you're at your most relaxed, and you think you're safe, you never are. Because you will always have that thing attacking you somewhere. Your mind, your heart. Being safe is your number one priority for the rest of your life after a parent dies. It's not about money or a job or a family or a career. It's about trying to block out the noise and the shame. And now a panic sets in. I light two cigarettes and smoke them both at the same time. I want to scream but there's just no sense. So I just sit there in the mud and smoke until his voice dies, crumbles into the late morning atmosphere. Fucking bastard. Still trying to get me after all this time. I don't even know how long it's been since he died. But it hasn't been long enough, that's for sure.

I get the camera ready and I trudge out into the middle of the river and I just start taking pictures. I'm not worried about focus or any of the technical aspects. I'm just taking pictures. And I get lost in it. Everything I see I just keep going, trying to get it all down, so maybe I can make a slideshow, a version of time that I can call mine and that nobody has the right to judge or lay criticism to. Because that's not how we should act. We should not take other people's things and call them their own. Like Dad did. Goddamn it. I can't get him out of my head now. It's like a ringing, a terrible song of fits and spasms. So I shoot faster. I do anything I can to not hear his voice berating me in that drunken slur as I have come to memorize. It's like a nerve. It's like I'm drowning in his wonderful ways. Like he's teaching me. Like I'm going to become him. Like I am the next worst person in the entire world.

Do this, do that.

You whore.

I didn't teach you to be like this.

You're not strong enough.

Have a drink.

Come on, have one.

I was too young to be a father.

We have no money to do anything you want.

Your Mom doesn't want me to do this.

I think you like her better.

You whore.

Why do you dress like that?

Just have one drink.

I'm going to be ok. I won't die.

I'll be your father forever.

You have to listen to me.

You're not good enough to carry this name, you fuck.

You. Whore.

I finally have enough of listening to that motherfucker's droning Irish bray so I put my earbuds in and I turn up *Midnight in America* as loud as possible and I feel the blood rush and I wind up punching the rocks that lay dead and dormant in the river. My hand is bleeding, and I realize I am way too violent for my own good so I take a picture of my bloody hand that drips red into the water and I follow the drops as they hit the clear and it's almost as relaxing as sleeping. I take a picture of my knuckles. I liken them to weaponry. I liken my entire body to a tank that will run through the competition. I guess he taught me something after all, the lousy asshole. And he's talking still through the delightful noise, I still hear the ringing through the music, the ringing, the ringing through the pictures, piercing through the nature I needed to embrace. Ringing.

I feel it in my pocket.

It's my phone. I have service out here?

I answer the phone with my bloody hand. I let the camera hang. I speak.

"Hello?"

"Bronwyn. It's Elaine."

elaine

"What?"

The service must have been awful. So I said it a little louder. "Bronwyn, it's Elaine."

There was a pause. I heard water somewhere. I hope she wasn't in the bathroom. Because this was awkward enough.

Finally, I heard, "Hi."

"Hello."

"What are you doing?"

I searched for the right words. Finally, I said, "I read your e-mail."

Another pause. I guess she was better insulting or judging people in person than through the phone. I heard her take several deep breaths, like she was in a race or a fight or something. Knowing her, it was probably the latter. But I was trying to do this with an open mind. It was rare for her, I guessed, to be so articulate and emotional. So I was being delicate. I wanted to do this right. Even though I didn't want anything to do with her, like I said, when I read her letter I figured that took a lot of guts to admit. So I remembered what Mom always told me. To hear people out. To give them second chances. I guess it's left over from the days I still went to Mass. So I went with it. I didn't have anything else to do. I would devote as much as time as I could to clear the air. Because I can't deal with grudges. Maybe I am weak. I still waited for a response and got none, so I clarified, "The one you sent late last night."

"Yeah, I know," she said. "I remember."

"I, uh...well, I really appreciated it."

"Good."

"It meant a lot."

"I'm glad."

"So, I guess what I'm saying is that, uh, I'm calling because I wanted to talk a little bit about it more."

"What's there to talk about?"

I wanted to be careful. She was a real hothead. "I think there's a little more to it than what you wrote to me."

"You know, this isn't a 'meet the author' type thing. I said I was sorry. And I am. And I guess that I shouldn't be so mad at you right now. I did tell you to call me, after all."

"That you did."

She sighed. I heard her grunt. "Forgive me. I was in the middle of an episode."

"You ask for forgiveness an awful lot."

"Sue me. I'm a terrible person."

"I'll be the judge of that." Even though I KNEW she was.

"That's cool. Judging's alright. Stereotypes are a real time saver." I heard the snap of a lighter and a deep hacking cough. I could never find the point of smoking. Why kill yourself daily when you've been given the chance to live a life for free? Didn't make any sense of me. But it's not an act of rebellion. It's a coping mechanism, I guess. So I let it slide. And I actually laugh at what she says, even though it's a horrible thing to say. There was a charm in it, oddly enough.

"Look, Bronwyn, I guess I have to apologize too."

"For what?"

"I kinda acted a little crazy myself. Last night."

"How?"

"Well, when you got in my face, I was ready to fight. And I'm ashamed to say it. I don't like to fight. I'm not that type of person."

"Hell, I'm glad you got in my face," she said after a few seconds. "That was the defining factor of me finally getting in touch with you."

"That I wanted to hurt you?"

"Yes!" She screamed. "My God, Elaine, that's what I was talking about last night. It came out wrong. I know it did. But I was pissed. And I'm glad you were. Because that right there is living life. You have to be angry. Being happy all the time, what the fuck do you learn?"

"You can learn lots of things being happy," I said, trying to defend myself. It was like I was talking to a professor or something. Even though she dressed like a goth, she sure was good at manipulating people and pulling people in certain directions of a conversation.

"Like what? Like Lennon was murdered but Michael Bolton was allowed to live?"

That one goes over my head a little, so I change the topic. "Look, Bronwyn. The point is that I almost hurt you. And I'm sorry about it. I'm not exactly as innocent as you think. I know you probably came up with some strong opinions during those months of support group, but in all honesty... I'm really not. I've had some problems."

"Dear, you're HUMAN. Say it out loud."

"I'm human."

"Good."

"So what?"

"So that means you're ALLOWED to have problems. In fact, Jesus, that's your RIGHT. But whatever. You'll feel better if I accept your apology, I know. So fine. I accept your unnecessary apology. As long as you truly and genuinely accept my completely necessary apology, then we're square."

"I do. I guess I can understand where you were coming from. I didn't exactly word it right, you know, what I said. I know I was stumbling over my words. But I meant what I said. And I guess that's what counts in the end, right?"

"Good. Yes. That's what counts. That you were honest. Great. Yahoo, yippee, and 23 skidoo. Then it's all fine. Do we need to talk about anything else?"

I didn't know what to say. A million different questions went through my head. Why do you act like that, then? How did your dad die? What do you do for work? Do you really know what love is or are you lying to me? What's your favorite band? Do you want to be friends? In the end, all I said, was, "Yes."

"Master of suspense here, Elaine Meadows. Yes. Ok. So what do you want to talk about? I know I'm being short. But I'm in the woods."

"What are you doing in the woods?"

"I'm a photographer. Ok, not really like a certified full time one. Amateur. Ok, yes, fine. You brought that up. I'm sorry I took a photo of you. I'll delete it right away. It's nothing sexual, I promise."

I let that go. "Why did you, anyway? Take a photo of me?"

"Because. I'm trying to document my life."

"Why?"

"Dumb question. Ok. Look. You need to understand something about me, while I have you on a mobile phone. Words are fickle. They can get clouded real fucking quick. But pictures? You can't change them much. Ok, maybe, if you're in Photoshop. But when you take them? That's real as shit. And you can't change that. Because you know what you saw. And that's a big teller of truth. More than just saying what you need to say. Word vomiting, that can be skewed and manipulated like hell if you tell the wrong person. And you standing there, looking like you were ready to box? Man. I was ready to shit. So I took a picture. BECAUSE THAT'S LIFE. Do you get it? That look in your face. That was badass. You looked like what's-her-name in that goofy ass movie where she kills all those people. Know what I'm talking about?"

I was a little stunned so all I said was, "You seem to be more culturally in tune more than me. I mean, I don't know the movie. I'm Catholic so that says a lot." And I didn't realize what I said until I heard the words. Why did I say that?

But she laughed. And I mean she laughed. A big bellowing gut laugh. So I guess that works. I appear better in her eyes and that's what matters in the end.

"Oh, Elaine. Thank you for that laugh. That was awesome. I mean, I needed that. I've had a shitty day so far."

Ask her questions, I thought. Get to know her. "So, Bronwyn, uh...look, I know this may be a little forward, but...what are you doing later tonight?"

"Probably chaos," she said.

I waited until she explained more. She didn't.

"Chaos?"

"A joke, Elaine. See Webster's."

"Ah. Well, I will then."

"What am I doing later tonight? Nothing. Why?"

"I thought maybe you would want to hang out. You know, clear the air more."

"How much more air is there to clear?"

"A lot. I mean. We're not in support group anymore. Because we kinda screwed that up."

"Yeah we did. That was fun."

"Well, fun wasn't the word I was looking for. But. I mean."

"You need a friend."

She got me there. I had no choice but to tell the truth. "Yes, I do." It hurt to admit it. But honesty was going to help me here. Nothing else.

"Well, you're in luck. I need a friend too."

"Do you?"

"Yes. And I think, Elaine, you proved yourself. You've shown yourself to this Irish bitch that you can handle a little of the ol' razzle dazzle. Know what I mean?"

That explains the odd accent. "I didn't realize this was a test."

"Everything in life is a test. Never forget that. So what am I doing later? Nothing. I guess your next move is to invite me somewhere. You don't want to go to your house because your folks - sorry, shit - Mom is there, and you're skeptical of introducing me to her so that's not going to work. So the only thing I can think of is like a diner or a bowling alley or a bar and I don't bowl because that's for losers with big muscles but I do drink so the diner doesn't work so I guess the bar is the best choice, right?"

"Uh, I'm only twenty?"

"Fuck. Ok. Diner, then. Am I right?"

I never fought this much in one simple conversation. I didn't see it going this far. I thought she would have hung up on me by this point by now. I'm also terrible at planning. "Yeah, that works. I guess. I have no problems with that?"

"Ok. Which one do you prefer?"

"Limerick, I guess? I can't stand Collegeville."

Another big bellowing gut laugh. "My god, Elaine. I think you're getting better and better by the minute. I'm damn fucking sorry I doubted you. Okay. What time?"

"I don't get done work until about five so like seven?"

"And where do you work?"

Oh man. I knew this was coming. "I answer the phones."

"Where? At the Pentagon? Why did that sound so pained and secret?"

"At a dentist's office. I'm working my way through school. I'm very part time."

"Nothing wrong with that. I work in retail. Okay? I know pain. Trust me. I'm off today so seven works for me. At Limerick. Fine. That's brilliant. They have good hot chocolate."

I had to agree with that. "Ok, I'll meet you there, then."

"Fine. So, is there anything else? Literally, anything else? Do you want to know anything about Bronwyn Sullivan? Any burning questions that can't wait?"

I detected a bit of sarcasm but I put up with it because that's just how her personality is. Don't take it personal. You made it this far. You can finish the conversation. You can do this. Don't be a pussy now. I hate that term, for the record. But sometimes it does accurately describe how you are acting. And I need to stop that if I'm going to be in Bronwyn's company. Because she seems like she'll eat me alive and spit me out and not give a fuck where I wind up.

"How did your father die?"

There was a pause. I immediately felt bad.

"Oh, God, Bronwyn. I'm sorry."

"It's fine. I might as well finally say it. I didn't tell any of those bastards at Church Group. He drank himself to death. Literally. His liver gave up. So did his wallet. I guess, maybe, two years ago, he's been gone? It was very tragic. God, I cry every night."

I detected sarcasm there, I know it.

"And your father," she said, "died how? If you did say it, I wasn't listening."

I sighed. "A drunk driver hit him. Killed. In an instant. No chance to say anything."

There was an extremely long pause. More uncomfortable than anything I could have ever imagined. It almost felt like death was sizing us up for a second there. Finally, she said, in a low whisper: "I'll see you at seven, alright?"

"Yeah, fine, that sounds fine," I stammered. And she hung up. And there ended the longest phone conversation of my life. Other than the boyfriend, of course.

I looked at the phone. I blinked. Everything became nonsensical and tough to follow. Did I say something that offended her? I guess I'll have to wait to find out. But she didn't sound too mad at me. I don't know. Maybe that was just how she was. I'll have plenty of time to figure it out. Maybe she's not that bad now that she confessed. That's a good sign. She's progressing. Look at the positives, Elaine. That's what God always said. But enough about Him. That's what I say. That's better.

I wasn't at work yet when I called her but I was getting ready to go in so I guess it was good when we hung up when we did. I needed to know all that before I went into work. I didn't want to scare her about my temper. I was being honest. I needed her to know everything because like I said, I cannot hold grudges. And since we've both been kicked out of support group, she needed to know every single thing. I needed to clear the air. That's the type of person I was raised into being. To teach. To educate. To have no secrets and to show people the beginning, the middle, and the ending of everything I am. At the diner tonight, she'll find out everything. And maybe we'll become friends. Mom will be proud. Dad, especially. He would be particularly proud. He would know everything I was doing would be for him in the long run. I needed to let go of the past, I guess. Bronwyn is right. I can't hang onto everything. I have to let go of something if I'm going to grow older.

I called the boyfriend quick before I went into work. I told him the whole Bronwyn saga finally because I didn't explain it fully the night before. He agreed with everything I said. He thought I was doing the right thing. He said I was being a good person. He said he wanted to hang out with me tonight but since I made plans with her he said he would bow out and see me later. I really pushed to see him but he was steadfast. He said this was something I had to do for myself. I thanked him for being lovely and I told him I loved him. He said he loved me.

He said he loved me.

bronwyn

I'm actually glad she called me because it gave me an awesome excuse to leave work early. It would cut down an already short shift even SHORTER and I was glad as hell to tell Stan in person so his face would get red and drop down into this goofy anagram of confusion. Sometimes, life can be sweet. And he did not disappoint when I went in there later:

"Hey, you, listen, I gotta leave by like six forty five. And I'm sorry but I cannot negotiate this, because it's kinda life or death. Like, I think someone from some terrorist group is coming to kill me, and I think that pretty much boils back down to the whole life or death aspect, don't you think so buddy?"

"Hey, Bronwyn, wait, what?" He's in the middle of cutting a box and he almost slips and slices his lousy finger with the cutter, which is about as sharp as a butter knife, but it's Stan, so he could probably fuck up a ketchup sandwich, given the tools.

"They're coming to take me away, ha, ha," I say, trying to be my most maniacal.

"Wait, aren't you supposed to close with - "

"Stan, you are a prince. A gentleman and a scholar. If you do not find true love at some point in your life, then I say it's a blight to all of female humanity. I would take you but I had mine sewn up a few years ago. Share a smoke with me later?"

"Bronwyn, you are touched."

And that's all that happens! Mr. By-The-Book doesn't even argue or ask later, as he's wont to do, because he's that type of person that must know the details of everything that happens to me because He Likes Me And I Do Not Like Him and he's too goofy to see the truth because he's sipping the Corporate Joy Juice. So we do this really awkward dance through the shift until I hightail it and I realize halfway through the diner and I didn't bring a change of clothes so she's going to know where I work and then I have to talk about that and there is not alcohol in the world to properly drown out the consciousness that I work in Retail, and there's no way out. I guess I just gotta remind her that I wanna be like Kevin Carter. But, for right now, I guess I must settle for this carousel, and all the horses? They're deadly. And badly painted. And it might be possible they want to kill me.

I pull into the diner and decide to have a quick smoke and think about what happened to me earlier in the woods. I look at my bloody hand and it looks like it got caught in a lawnmower or a dog attacked it. I'm proud of my mutilated self and at the same time, I'm proud of how well I can fix myself. Because flesh and bone is really hard to fix. Some people can do it very well and others can't do it all. But I know how to do it, and that makes me a special case. People will run to me later in life and they will ask me to help them. That's what I will do. Maybe. It depends on how much I hate people in a few years. Probably more. Probably a LOT more. If things don't wind up the way I want them, I may just wind up disturbed and easily volatile. There's a sense of security in that, I think. If my photography doesn't wind up making the world cry, if they do not fall to their knees and shake the ground with their love, then I might just jump off a building and take any beating hearts I acquire somehow along the way. It's noble as shit. It's the only way to die - to hate life the entire time. That way, you know it wasn't all for nothing. It has to be all for something, right? All of this. Surgeries and pill popping and getting older. Learning how to write and learning how to kiss and learning how to fuck. It all has to be for us. Even though we don't know what to do with it. Fuck. I sound like Dad now. I shake my head, get the cobwebs out, try to start over. I have to remember to go into this with a positive aura. I actually want her to get along with me now, for some reason. I'll find out when it's too late.

I guess she's running late so I go into the diner and get a table. I hate waiting for someone else when you're in a restaurant. You have to sit there and twiddle your goddamn thumbs and tell the waitress, "no, wait, there's someone else, I guess I'll just wait to order when they come" which sucks because I really do want a hot chocolate. But I'll be polite. So I sit and I start to write on the napkin they left me and I'm in the middle of a doodle when I feel a shadow start to cover me, and I never look up when that happens because I'm led to believe that it's a nightmare or a hipster at that point.

"Hey," I hear in a voice I recognize.

I draw for three more seconds until I look up. And it's Elaine, all right. Now, in all the times I ever saw her at that group, she always dressed real smart-like. Nice shirts, nice pants, like she looked like a college girl at Vassar or NYU. But now I think she was dressing to impress me which is completely wrong because she's not being true to herself. She's wearing a cinder grey band t-shirt (I will not embarrass her by mentioning the band's name, but just know that they suck and I wish fire and brimstone upon them) and cargo pants and her hair is down. It was always up before. Like I said, college girl. Kinda like an old secretary or a librarian in a black and white movie. But now she looks like she's ready to join Kristen Stewart somewhere. Perhaps that's too harsh of a reference, but I had to get my point across. And you can tell she doesn't know what to say to me in person now, because our previous two conversations were "hey, I'm going to beat the fucking shit out of you" and "hey, I can't see you, I'm hiding behind a phone". So I guess I better be nice and lead her by the hand out of this dark patch.

"Elaine," I say, trying an American accent for a change.

She smiles. I have achieved. "Hi. How are you?"

"I'm talking to a giant," I say.

She looks me at quizzically.

"It means you should sit."

She nods her head and sits, looks at the paper advertisement placemat (FREE ABORTION? CALL US AT XXX-XXX-XXXX), and then stares back at me, all red in the face.

"Why do you look like you just pissed on a rug?"

"You're very to the point, aren't you," she says.

"There's no sense wasting time in this life. Get to the point. Say what you need to say. There's plenty of other things I can think of wasting my time on. Use short, clipped sentences. Be honest. Be direct. Be creative." I show her my napkin artwork. "Do you like it? I drew it for you." It's a picture of a horse attempting to climb a tree. I never said I was a good artist. I may be known to fuck shit up, but that's about it.

She laughs and she takes it. "It's not exactly Black Beauty, is it?"

"It's Barbaro. When he was still alive."

Her face contorts, since it's a joke that some people take a little too seriously. Get over it, I say. Not to her but you know.

"I will cherish it," she says, and folds it and puts it in her pocket. The waitress comes by so now finally I can order my goddamn hot chocolate. She would like a green tea. Certainly, she says. I will return with your drinks. Will we be getting food? Elaine looks at me. I haven't eaten all day and I'm not going to begin now so I wave her off. Elaine looks at the menu for a half of a second, but debates against it and waves her off. And that's it for the preliminaries. There's going to be no more outside interference. So it's time to get to the point of the whole night.

"Elaine," I say after we are alone, "what are you trying to do to do here?"

She looks at me and says, "What do you mean?"

"I know you don't like me. At all. And a small part of you feels insanely guilty for some reason for what you did yesterday. And I know we talked on the phone earlier, but. You can lie like hell on the goddamn phone because no one sees your face. And the face? That tells everything. Window to the soul. So right now, directly to me, Elaine. Let's talk. Let's not hide what you really want to say to me. If you wanted to apologize to me and mean it, you wouldn't have asked to see me. So there's something else there. So go on. I want to know. Because, as you will soon know, I've had a lot of people tell me the wrong thing in my life, and quite frankly. I'm pretty fucking tired of it."

I'll give her credit - she matched my gaze the entire time. That's tough to do. Not a lot of people have done it. I meant what I said about faces. They mean everything. They are the beginning, the end, the fire, the ice, the explosion and the crater in the land it makes afterward. It's easy to see the bullshit. And if she's going to be a part of my life, I need to know she's genuine. I won't abide by liars and bastards anymore. Call me crazy, but I need a shield now.

After the bullets that have been sent my way in this short life.

She looks around for a second, which I don't know why she does, but I guess it's to confirm there's a slight comfort here. Then she speaks with a dead hum that almost, but not quite, scares me a bit: "I almost killed you last night."

I didn't say anything. I just waited.

"I could have if I wanted to. And I was close."

I was waiting to see if she was just still talk. But she didn't retract. She kept on me. And I saw something swimming in her eyes. Hurt. Pain. A song that had no proper ending. A knife sharpened, waiting for skin to stab. A normal human being with a normal human life, once whole, now torn like cheap paper. So I wasn't going to fuck around with her anymore. She had her chance to be civil and this has been going on too long. I could be with real friends or making more money.

"So fucking kill me, then," I whispered.

"Don't say that," she said.

"Why not? Remember what I said about wasting time? Don't waste mine. So make your move.

Go ahead. I'll let you have the first move. If you're stupid to make it."

But she didn't move. She just sat there. And she was trying to transform into something non-human but I wasn't buying it. But she kept her voice steady, like a rock. She was doing better than most people with ol' Bronwyn. So far, only her and my Dad made it this far. And I hate to say this, but I almost have to respect her. Even if she did have a death wish.

"I almost killed a girl when I was younger," she began. "In high school. In gym class. We were changing afterwards. She made a comment about my tits. She said she would suck them if they were big enough. And if they weren't good enough for her, they wouldn't be good enough for anyone. So I walked up to her. And she said to me that she just said she wasn't interested in me. So back the fuck up. So I turned around to leave. And then something in me snapped. She said something else. I don't know what. But I turned. And I punched her in her face. No slap. None of that bitch shit. And I grabbed her by her fake-ass fucking blonde hair. And I took her and I slammed her head against the locker. Someone ran and got the teacher. But in those few seconds of freedom, I made sure she never said a goddamn word again. I slammed her head against the locker. She was trying to apologize to me. But I did it again. And some of my friends were trying to pull me off. I don't remember even saying words but they said I was. And I was begging her to say something else. Finally they got me off. She was bloody. She said she was joking. And I got real close to her and I said I don't believe in jokes. And I said she was lucky that I didn't stick my fucking tit in her mouth for her to suck. And then I walked away. The school cop came. I was almost arrested. Charges were almost pressed. But she didn't press. She let it go. She said she was sorry. She said she would never do that again. She changed into a better person. But that didn't change how I felt. Every time I saw her afterwards, I wanted to break her back. I almost killed her. Someone. A person." And right when she finished her story, the waitress brought us our drinks. And she looked down at her tea and she put the bag in the cup and she poured in some sugar and as she did so, she looked up at me and it was like she never even said what she said. She turned into The Church Group Elaine.

Instead of The Real Elaine I just saw. I knew this was real.

And I didn't move. I sat there for a minute. I stirred my hot chocolate around and I let the accurate amount of time pass until I said what I needed to say. She knew that a moment existed too, and she wouldn't dare say another word because what she was perfect enough to be remembered by all for a long time. I looked out of the window. I tried so hard to search for the right thing to say. Because she just showed me what her heart looked like. And it wasn't a muscle.

It wasn't anything like that.

elaine

My brain was dead. I relived the blood. I heard the screaming. I felt the scraping of skin. I felt the bitch's voice overtake me. I tried to dull the noise. I drank tea. I looked out the window. I tried to remember the therapist's methods to calm down. I hated it. I missed Dad. I bit my tongue. I was sitting across from someone who pretended to be someone she wasn't. I made a mistake. I need to teach love. I can't be here. I can't be anything. I am nothing. I should have been with the boyfriend tonight instead. My brain, my lousy dead brain. I will put it into the trash when I get home. I heard her scream. I realized I used words I shouldn't have. I need to go. I need to drive. I must become something else. I have to be a better dream than the one I think I am now.

"I know that's not bullshit," she finally said.

I waited. Her turn to talk now. Not mine.

"Thank you, Elaine."

"For what?"

"For telling me that. And being honest with yourself enough to finally tell someone that. That should have been told months ago. In front of those fucks at church."

"Why? What do you mean?"

"So people can finally understand the rage about you losing your father."

"But this happened way before he died - "

"Doesn't matter. That don't mean anything. It meant solely that the rage you felt then is the rage you felt now. And you're afraid to show it now because it might mean someone will die. And you don't want to do that because you don't want any more people to die. So you hold it in. And you only go there to talk about things that don't involve how you're feeling. You change it around so your truth doesn't come out. You project something else because you don't think anyone else will really understand what you mean. And you took offense to me and me only because I actually had the balls to call you out on it. That's why you got mad. Because I almost ruined the gig. And now I know why you did all of it. Because you're dangerous. And you really would have killed me, I know."

Son of a bitch.

She's totally right.

I took a deep breath to try to calm down, to return to normal. I needed to be normal. I needed to go back to the person that I knew, that I dealt with daily.

"But Elaine, there's one thing you don't know about me."

I took a sip of tea. "What's that?"

"I would have given you one hell of a fight." And she showed me a cut and recently bloody hand. Along with her bloody forehead from yesterday, I believed it. It all made sense. She hurts herself rather than others. She was a general in some war that had no other fighters except herself. She hated a society where everyone was peaceful. Which is why she wanted to fight with me so bad. Because she needed something to fuel her along, to get her through the day, because her own life was so banal and empty.

"And now what you need to know about me, Elaine, is that I kicked my Dad in the fucking head while he lay on my living room floor calling me a whore and for calling my mother a slut," she said. "About how I was beautiful and about how he would finger me if I wasn't his daughter and how I wasn't strong enough to carry his name. And he died cursing everything under the sun. And I watched him. And it was brilliant." She wore a sick smile. "And that was my experience. I beat the shit out of him because he deserved it and because I loved him and I wouldn't want anyone else doing it because they didn't know him like I knew him. The beating meant something."

I swallowed hard.

"And he died happy because he knew he accomplished his mission. No one liked him. At all. Ever. At any point. Well, I guess my mother did because I'm here. So I guess we're fucked up enough, aren't we? But I had that rage at him. That was all him. He did that to me. Was your dad perfect? Was he everything you wanted him to be?"

"Yes," I said quietly. Hold back the tears, please. Don't cave now. It won't be worth it. Cry later when you have no one else to go to. You have a friend here. Don't do anything wrong.

"What did he do?"

"He loved me," I said.

"He loved me, too. He just didn't know how to do it RIGHT."

And then I started to cry. My facade was slipping. I was making an ass of myself. Pull the tough girl act only to fall apart moments later. Way to go, Elaine. Fool the people that don't matter but give up when the timing is everything. I quick wiped them away and prayed that she didn't notice it.

"Elaine," she said sharply.

I looked at her. I held it in well enough.

"Do not, under any circumstances, give the fuck up."

I nodded. I let my head hang afterwards.

"No, you don't know. Don't give me a courtesy nod. LOOK at me."

I looked back up and I wanted to say something smart but I didn't have the courage to do so. I held my tongue in.

"I'm sorry your dad is dead. Ok? What was his name?"

It had been a while since I actually said his name out loud. It was going to be weird. I looked at Bronwyn hard and summoned up the power to say: "Joseph."

"Joe, huh?" She said and nodded. "Ok. I'm sorry he's gone."

"Don't say Joe."

"Ok. I won't."

"No one calls him that."

"I'm sorry."

"It's ok."

We sat in a silence for a while as I looked around where I was, taking it all in. I didn't ask for any of this. I asked for an easy life. Just like everyone else had. A family. Whether it was normal or not. I just wanted stability. I just wanted a building, a structure. Something that was going to last me a very long time, not just something that was temporary and shoddy.

"So you thought my thing about the structure was all bullshit."

I caught her in the middle of a sip. She looked confused for a second and then she became aware of it. "Hmm, not all of it. Actually, that was probably the most truthful thing you said. I can totally buy into that."

"So why did you - "

"Because that whole part about staying the way you were and not wanting to change into a new person. That part was just crazy. Of course you want to be a new person. Because that's what you want to do and because what you need to do. Staying the same only makes you insane. You need to become someone else. Otherwise, the death just eats you up. You can't go on living those parts over and over again. It makes you sick. It makes you just want to curl into a ball and not do anything productive or relevant ever again."

"Like how?"

"Look at me. Do you think I always dressed like this?"

"No. So why do you?"

"Because. If you spend your whole life staying in the same time period, you will learn and experience nothing. Not one goddamn thing." She finished her hot chocolate.

"I never said I would - "

"But you kinda did, Elaine. You were content there for a while. But here's the harsh truth that Chad or any of those other dingle-dicks will never tell you. You need to let your father go."

That floored me for some reason. I downed the tea. It became hard to breathe. How could I ever do that? Why would I ever want to do a thing like that?

In the middle of my thoughts, she repeated it for emphasis. "You need to let your father go. Period."

"That doesn't seem like a good idea," I said. "My mother still thinks he's going to come back."

"You don't think that," she said.

"No. But I don't want to forget him."

"I'm not saying forget him. You can never forget him. Hell, I won't forget mine. But letting go? Totally different. He doesn't rule your life anymore. Sorry, but he doesn't."

"I never said he was," I said with anger.

"You don't have to. It's in you. The way you act."

"Bronwyn - " I started to say in a loud voice.

"I'm trying to help you," she said through gritted teeth. "Keep your voice down."

The waitress came by and she asked us if we wanted more of both and we both said yes. She took our cups away and we were left with nothing to hide behind.

I had never met anyone like Bronwyn before. She was pissed off at the world. And maybe she had a reason to be. I would never know the full story and I didn't even know if I wanted to. But there was truth to it all. She really felt everything that she said. Her words had sting, had bite to them. Like she was not well educated to anything important in the world other than to talk, and to bring reality to people's dreams. I couldn't see her doing anything that was going to be peaceful or even liked. But I could tell that she meant what she said, and that was enough for her, so it would have to be good enough for me and everyone else that chose to interact with her. Because she wasn't changing. She was who she was. And I guess I had no choice but to respect that. I didn't like her making accusations the way she was. But maybe she was trying to teach, like I wanted to. But she seemed like she was teaching hate. Like she wanted to destroy instead of mend. I wanted to bring people together. But she was trying to make everyone else alienate themselves and not accept what they really wanted to do. I think I'm over thinking everything, but I'm starting to think that this was a gigantic mistake. I wanted to call the boyfriend and tell him what was going on, just to hear what he thought of it. But I couldn't back out now. I had to ride this out. I couldn't run. She knew who I was. She knew almost everything about me now. I had no legs to run with.

The waitress came back and gave us fresh drinks. We did the same routine as before. Finally, I spoke.

"I can't forget my father entirely," I said. "That may work for you but it will not work for me."

"Fine," she said. "You have to live around it. As best as you can. That's the only way to cope."

"So how do I do that?"

"First off, you can't go around threatening to kill people."

I actually laughed at that. She did, too, after a while.

"Second, you need to find what you love to do, and don't give up. What do you like to do outside of work? Like, your hobby?"

"I always liked exploring, hiking," I said after a sip. "I like examining abandoned places."

"Good, me too," she said. "I told you I want to be a photographer. So there we go. We both have outside passions. That's what's important. Do you see anyone? Are you doing it with someone?"

I didn't feel that she needed to know that I was, so I lied. "No, I'm not."

"Ok, well, then, we need to change that."

"I'm not really looking," I said after a brief pause.

"Ok, fine, then you're not. But you need to find what you love and do that more than anything else. Ok, so you explore. Here's my point. Do what you love and try to forget the fact that they ever opposed it."

"They?"

"They, your parents. They always oppose. Hell, my Mom hates what I do. She can't stand the fact that I smoke and drink and listen to music that sounds like two dogs fighting. Maybe not dogs. Babies. Hyenas. Whatever."

"You really listen to that stuff?"

"It blocks everything out perfectly, the times when you need it to the most. Go home. Go to YouTube. Listen to Modern Life Is War. You'll understand that."

I made a mental check to do so, but I had a feeling I wouldn't enjoy that. I like things that are more serene and it sounded too angry. "So what then?"

"Go against the norm for a while, and then you'll figure it out, trust me."

Some time passed. She answered a text message from someone and I acted like I had one too but I was really checking my e-mail to see if I got anything from work. I went to say something, but I stopped myself. I felt like I was overstaying my welcome, which was incredibly silly but at the same time, was probably the perfect way to describe how this all felt. Like I was intruding on her at home. Like everywhere she went was home, only because she seemed like she was in complete control. I began to trust her for some reason. Finally I said, "Thank you."

She finished her hot chocolate and fidgeted it for a bit afterwards, like she had somewhere else to go. "For what?"

"For helping me."

She shrugged. "You showed me character. And honesty. I felt like you deserve to know how life really is when a loved one dies. I can always teach you more."

"I want you to."

"You mean," she said after a beat, "you want to do this again?"

"I do. I'm sorry I doubted you. I feel like you're smarter than half the people I know."

"That can't be saying a lot."

And I laughed. It was infectious. She giggled too.

"I'm serious," I said after a pause.

She rifled through her bag to get her wallet. I wasn't going to argue. "I don't know, Elaine. You might want to kill me."

I suddenly felt horrible.

"I'm kidding, Jesus," she said to break the tension. "I know you're a tough crazy mama. Look. Ok. Here's the deal. I work tomorrow, it's no good. But the next day? What day is that? Don't matter. If you really want to hang out with me, you can."

"I would like that," I said. I meant it, too. So we made plans to do so. And we both paid and we left. And on the drive home, I couldn't stop thinking about what she said about faces.

It was enough to make me think twice.

bronwyn

I sat in the car, waiting for her to leave first. I almost couldn't believe what I was seeing. Elaine. That girl, presented to me in two different packages. One normal, and one just...not what I was imagining in my head.

Was she really for real?

Finally she backed up and she waved at me and she drove off into the night. And she went back to her little cave of mystery and her little balls of anger and her stories full of hurting people and wanting to do what's right. It was so odd. I couldn't imagine someone being that conflicted, dreaming of doing the correct thing, pretending to be so moral, when underneath, there was this complete world of...what was the right word? Pain? Who even knew? Who could even guess it? I felt very bad for her. I knew that there was nothing I could really do to fix it. I wanted to, but at the same time, I felt like I would drive myself nuts if I were to reach in there and do for her what I did for myself. Because that shit took time, patience, and a LOT of alcohol. A lot of daydreaming. And I barely made it through that myself.

I smoked a cigarette as I sat in the car a little longer. I had nowhere else to go. It was fast becoming the story of my life. A young girl with a whole universe to commandeer and not one stop along the way that will make her feel loved. Not one piece of shelter that will make her want to go to sleep, not one roof that she can go under that will make her feel like she is fighting in a war. I just couldn't get the conversation out of my head. I replayed it. I look for nuances, flaws, holes, bad logic, clichés, anything that gave me any sort of indication that she was putting on a show. And I couldn't come up with anything. I would need assistance in trying to sort this mess out. I knew just the thing.

I drove over to the closest bar and I walked in and immediately got the same stare that I always get whenever I walk into a place like that - girl, what are you doing here? Most of where I go is frequented by older, "tough" men with badly done tattoos and thinning beards and wildly out of fashion t-shirts as they grasp their Lites like it is their grail, their only reason to get out of bed (well, that, and the half a boner they get when they wake up in the middle of the night, and that's only thanks to errant daydreams and hopes that are no longer relevant or attainable) and they look at me like I'm some sort of lesbian with an art degree that can't hold her own in a dive. And I have shown them before. I'm here to carve my own slice of the pie. They see that I'm in the mood for blood, baring my teeth, that I currently have an edge, so they make their judgments and raise their eyebrows and I take a table by myself in the corner and the only other woman in the bar (the waitress, of course) exchange high-fives and I order my drink (like you need to know what it is) and as I wait for it, I tap my fingers just like my Dad did, and my heart starts to hate things, just like Dad did. He'd be so proud. His own little clone, born and ready to do exactly what he did. Only I'm smarter.

I people watch. I admit it, I too. And I do hate them but at the same time I appreciate them all for being little clones of people that they never wanted to be. You grow up and as you wake up more and more, you say, "I can never be like this person". And then you do. It's flawless how well you transform into them. You inherit the quirks and you gain all of those dirty little movements and the next thing you know, you are. And it's too late to change it. It's just something that happens. When you're a kid in school, they feed you that bullshit. *Aww, honey, you can be anything you want to be! Anything you want to. Whatever you want to be, you can be the president, you can be an astronaut, you can be ruler of the world. You can do it! You really can!* And now I can finally say to all those teachers: go fuck yourselves. Liars, one and all. At least cigarette companies PRINT it on the box that you're going to die if you do too much of it. All those people oughta be hung by their thumbs for lying to you. I could never be President. There's people who oppose that kind of shit, you know. And then there's the people who witness something terrible in their lives and strive to fight against it. Like feminists. And I say that's a load of crap, too. People have actually come up to me, real people, and say, "Bronwyn, you could fight for a really good cause." Yeah, for who? For myself? Wish in one hand, crap in the other, see what fills up first. I'm too busy fighting for myself, twenty four hours a day seven days a week, to be bothered what happens with the REST of the already screwed human race. I can't stand them. There's like this unwritten rule that you have to fight for that automatically if you're a woman. And I say no. Because most of the feminists I know (the ones that I put up are usually the ones that fall in that category) are not feminists for two simple reasons: one, they're the type that refuses to fight HONESTLY for the cause so they just do Facebook links of articles that they're too busy to read and get mad when someone accurately calls them out on their bandwagon faith and two, the ones who date guys that HATE feminists, because they feel "safe" in their "faith" to not fight, and besides, why would a feminist want to date the enemy, anyway? I get my drink. I down it. She's awesome enough to bring two without me asking. This is my type of world, where drink flows freely, where I don't have to worry about getting my head bashed in, where black spots become erased more and more with my thoughts, where I can finally win a battle or two and not worry about getting burned. Because you know, I'm a delicate little fluffy flower who totally wants to hang out with you sometime. I start to write that little rant down in my diary of which I now carry with me everywhere, solely because you never know when someone is going to do something that pisses you off.

But, back to my point. Being someone you do not want to be. It's going to happen. Get over it. And I see it in Elaine now. She's going to be the complete opposite of her dad. Because he sounded like a real swell guy from what's she said about him. And that's totally well and good. I'm happy for her that she had the type of father that I always wanted to have. Ok, I'll admit it, I'm jealous. And I don't typically feel that way. But I will say it now because my defenses are down and I have nothing to lose. But she's going to lose her well-intentioned fight to be the person she wants to be. She just is. I mean, I don't see her taking over the world. I don't see her fighting for good causes. Maybe for a while. But she's going to see the darkness in her and it's going to win. And I need to tell her that. Because if she finds out how I find out, she's in a world of trouble.

I start to write furiously. I'm taken over by a need to shout but I hold it in. There's shitty music playing and people are staring at me and I truly don't give a fuck. I go to light a cigarette but the waitress stops me. I tell her this place always allowed it, but she points to a new sign, literally a day old brand new sign, that you can't smoke inside anymore. So I just let it hang from my lips and she shrugs and there's nothing she can do about it. She's goddamn right she can do nothing about it. So in compensation, she brings me another drink. Hey, fine by me. I got nothing to do anyway except complain. It's early yet. I try to keep writing but I keep getting distracted by Elaine's problem. So I change gears. I start writing about her. I have to help her. I can't let her go down the exact same road that I went down. Maybe the same county. But not the same road. Because there's way too many problems down that way. She's too fragile. She wouldn't be able to handle it. I can handle anything. But she can't. She thinks she's can. She's still in that stage where she wants everything to be fine. And nothing is ever fine, ever, ever, not ever or never, not even for a single solitary second. Keep fooling yourselves.

I'm thinking in pictures because the drink is too good. The music is not what I want it to be. And Dad's here somewhere. This would be his place. But I manage to forget him for a bit, which is nice. I keep writing until the pen runs out of ink. I can't believe it. For a second there, I actually laugh so I scribble like a madman and sure enough, it's deader than some child actor's career. I stand up and I almost get knocked down on my ass. I haven't been here that long already, haven't I? God. Must be stronger drinks, must be bigger glasses. But not my fault. I stumble up to the counter and everyone's too engrossed in their retarded baseball game. I can't stand that jock horseshit. Let's hit a ball and chase after it and then afterwards in the locker room, we'll all pump each other until we're blue in the faces and then we'll all sing songs afterwards. Finally, I tap "shave and a haircut" on the counter until I get the bartender's attention. BE NICE TO YOUR BARTENDERS. They're God's true soldiers of destiny and happiness. And tip them, too. Sound advice I will teach my daughter one day. God. What a thought. And I laugh at that and then I remember he's waiting for me to speak my wonderful clouded drunk thought. Not drunk. Tipsy. Don't give up the keys yet.

"Oh, I need a pen," I say.

He stares at me like it's a drink he doesn't know. I provide sign language. Somewhere, one of the mongoloids crowded around the bar titters like a schoolgirl. Up yours, I think. He comes back with a pen with blue ink. I don't play around with that stuff. This ain't no game. I can tell it's blue because of the cap. I'm attentive.

"I need black ink," I say.

"This ain't Staples."

"Yeah, but if you can root around there, one is bound to come up."

He keeps looking. Finally, I feel a tap on my shoulder. I spin and it's the waitress. She hands me hers. I take it and I nod and I shoot a look at the bartender and I say in my best brogue, "The luck of the Irish. Thank you darling." And she smiles and rolls her eyes and I go back to my table and I realize they're all looking and I think to them all, eat shit, you dogs. You think you're all so great, like you're the morning dew. Well, think again, because you're not that, you're just all piss. I fart in not just your general direction, but all directions. So suck it.

Another drink. It flows into me quite easily and my skin and soul will not break. I crawl back to my table where I sit and I will continue to get weird stares. Fuck them if they've never seen a beautiful girl that uses her brain instead of her legs and her tits. That's the whole point of living. I'm writing about Elaine, I'll admit it. And why not? What else am I going to do all night, living here in Suck City? All in black ink, permanent and multi-functional and damning and systematic. And under the influence of wonderful alcohol, I will sit and keep my cool and I will have nowhere to go and I will have voices to avoid all night because they are nothing, I am better than it. It's easy to call yourself superior when you know all around you is nothing.

And my heart starts to pour out all the things I wanted to say to a younger version of myself, if I only knew of them then. These are non-removable things; they burn a tremendous fire, and the old me is sitting there on a wooden bench in my mind, tampering with something unclassifiable, her mind blown with the knowledge that always escaped her.

She is almost all static now, awash in a glowing light in which she knows nothing of source or volts or amperes, she is sitting smiling, taking it all in, gleaming with a new comfort that she never otherwise knew of or even imagined. She is angelic in a pathetic way, and her ears are wide open, because I talk to her now, the sound barging its way with fight. Listen, I write and say. There's something here. It's an amazing show of blood that answers all mysteries, shows you all of any river and sky and tree and land that never made sense before, and it's all in my hand, one that I will not give to just anyone. If they want it, I tell her, they will have to cut it off and it won't be worth much anyway.

I'm drunk.

Time to admit it now.

It's wonderful to breathe a new air and to have tears that aren't falling yet.

Someone's tapping me on the shoulder and I must have said something like fuck because I have angry eyes getting angrier jumping all over me, tough like razor-wire, but belonging to weak-spined men with small dicks and idiotic dreams.

Someone tells me to get out.

You're all fools. And I remember hitting solid wood, but no one touched me. And I touch my head and there's blood. How about that? I say. Damn thing. Keeps coming back, even when I get eight hours of sleep.

elaine

I drove and I became afraid. I sounded like the biggest bitch in the world and I didn't want to be like that. I wanted to be my honest self - my whole innocent self. I mean, I guess I was being honest - I really did try to hurt someone badly once. And I was telling her how I felt the other night. But it all came out so wrong. I'm pretty sure I messed up the perfect opportunity to be so normal for once. And she was different, yes, and extremely off-putting, but at the same time, I wanted to make a clear impression to her, that I am able to withstand any judgment and attack. Because I need to be that person now, obviously, if I want to make it in this world. But I wasn't thinking about her now. I was just trying to focus on the road long enough to get somewhere without crashing. I can't end up like he did.

So I pull over for a while in a gas station parking lot and I start to look around at things and I realize I can't really recognize them right away because I'm trying to associate them under a separate category than I have before. Life without him, thinking without him, not comparing him with anything, trying to move on without him, picking up all pieces without him, finally trying to rid my mind so I can be happy without him. It was a terrible thing to do. And she actually suggested I do it. And she meant every single world, which was the scary thing. She said it with such authority, with such...command. I didn't know what to do. I didn't know what Mom was going to do. It was going to be the worst time of my life, when it's supposed to be the happiest time, when I'm on my own and figuring out what I am going to do. I wanted to die. I don't mind admitting that. But I knew I was not going to do anything about it, so I pushed the urge right out of my head and pulled out of the station and went back right onto the road. I started to drive to the boyfriend's house. I needed some sanity. And he really is the perfect example.

I surprised him, I know, by pulling up out of nowhere, but he saw me and came out and immediately I started crying when I saw him and I fell into his arms as he sat in my passenger seat. And I let it all out. I won't say what I said again but needless to say it's pretty much everything you know already, and he just stroked my arm and played with my hair and did everything that cheers me up and just listened. He never tried to interrupt, he never tried to put in his own opinion. He just sat there and let me talk and it was the best thing that could have happened to me. Because I'm one of those people who just need to be heard. I'm a terrible listener, I admit this. And that's why he truly is my better half - he's everything I'm not. I told him all about Bronwyn, about her blood, about her "fuck everything" approach, how she seemed fit to destroy life if she had the proper tools. And I told him that I wanted to kill her and maybe that I still do, but it's only because she was right. And that's when he finally jumped in and said, Elaine, she's not right. She's not right at all. She's trouble and she's going nowhere with her life.

She seems like she's the kind of person that wants to ruin other people's chances for success because she lost her own chances, and I'm not going to stand by and let her do that to you because you don't deserve that. She's weird and she's not good for you. And I nodded and cried into his chest. He was right. I just didn't know, I kept repeating. And he kissed me on the head and just said, I know. It's been a tough few days. Let's go inside and try to forget the whole thing. And for once, I remember thinking against that. I didn't want to forget it. I wanted to keep talking about it so we could find an ANSWER. But I was tired so I agreed. I just didn't want to spend all night in the car.

I'm not trying to say that I didn't want his love. Because his love is one of the purest things I've ever had the pleasure of touching. I didn't think it was entirely attainable years ago when we started, but as time wore on, it became stronger and stronger. And when Dad died, I thought he would have ran because then he wouldn't have to deal with the burden of having a wounded girlfriend and dating someone who was down one parent. But he stayed and gave no indication he was going to leave, even though he had every right and chance to do so. And he held my hand through every trip to the funeral home and all throughout the funeral and he gave me my space when I asked and he read my thoughts when I was too exhausted to speak. He was a rock. And he could have run. But he didn't. And that's when I knew that love was completely and utterly true. I wouldn't know if I could do the same, though. I always go back to him being afraid I'm missing my Dad because then it wouldn't create the perfect family in the future.

Because ever since then, I've lived with that fear and it keeps me up at night. My kids won't have a grandfather, at least on my side. And that sucks because they didn't deserve that void. They're going to ask questions and look at pictures and I'm going to relive it all over again. I always wanted that perfect family from day one, so everyone could get together years in the future and you could see the generations all lined up, and it would be happy. Even in the face of a terrible, cruel world, at least everyone you loved that loved you back would be there, regardless of age or belief. And now one is missing. And he happens to be the most important one of all. And I wake up in the middle of the night, gasping, because I dream of photographs that are torn or burnt or that's missing his face and I know it's not coming back. I explained this all to him one night and he said he wasn't leaving me. He said he was going to marry me and that he would be the best father for our kids and that he had no plans to do anything else. And that helped, for a while. But it doesn't completely erase my thought. It only mends it briefly, holds it in, and I guess that's all I can ask for, given that people have it far worse than me. There's always a victim that's worse off. I need to stop complaining. I need to embrace what I have.

And that's what I'm starting to get tired of. I need this, I want this, I have to do this, I have to stop doing this, I need, I need, I need. It's getting tiring. Is there a way to stop being so selfish, to just stop for one second and feel what you need to feel and do nothing with that feeling? That's the most beautiful thing in the world to me. When you can watch a fire and not worrying about what damage can bring, that you just can watch and knowing full well that it will never touch you, it will never come near your heart unless it's a thought you bring in to your life yourself. And that's what this world as a whole needs to do. Let's appreciate, let's create instead of wanting to hurt yourself, wanting to make yourself look like a fucking problem, being a problem instead of becoming a solution, like Bronwyn. But as much as she disgusts me, she lingers, she refuses to go away. I don't know what it is about people like her, but they find people like me, and they just want to latch on and suck them dry. She wants to be like them so bad because she forgets how to be herself. But maybe she is herself and she hates it so that's why she saw someone like me and saw that they could be even halfway remotely successful so they want to be in my aura and see what's it's like to live life with open eyes. I don't even know. I feel myself becoming horrible and unliked. And that's what she went through and she wants me to do it too.

People like her make me sick.

But I need to change gears.

I walk into the house with the boy and his parents greet me warmly. I'm so grateful for the change in atmosphere right now. It's warm and welcome and I feel like a different person sometimes being in this house because everything is so open and so free from the bad shit. They have everything I ever dreamed of for myself and the boyfriend knows this so I'm never going to have it away from my life from this point on. They're sitting on the couch sipping wine and they don't offer me one because they're doing the right thing which I totally respect and we all sit for a while and laugh at really bad jokes and just catch up with each other. He's an only child so they are able to devote all the time in the world to him and what he likes, which is really cool. There's a way to be a helicopter parent without constantly flying and I want that to be me. They must teach me their secrets one day because I really want to know. My mother is a good mother. And I want to be like her but I want to even better, and I know that sounds horrible, but I just think that's the day's sadness washing over me, but it's soon forgotten, and hours pass at that house, cuddling and watching movies and finally they go to bed, leaving just me and him. And if you think it's going to go like that, it's not. Not every night alone has to be spent like that. I mean, I never complain when it does, but tonight's just not the night. You have to respect the boundaries. If you don't, there's no hope for you.

So like a total romantic he dims the lights (of course) and he comes back to the couch and he turns the volume down on the television but keeps it on just for a perfect background. And he starts to talk about his day because honestly it is his turn and I listen and even though he is being completely okay, I almost want to bring up my problems again because his problems are not problems, they're just nuisances. I have better scars than him. Not a damn thing ever went wrong in his life and now he's trying to tell me that he's got some situations he can't handle and I just nod and be loving but I almost want to scream at him because he knew how upset I was earlier and he's just trying to forget about it all. I know I sound like a total crazy person psycho right now and I don't know why because I'm really not like that. I just have a lot of things on my mind but all of a sudden he pushes them out of my head with a few really well-placed words.

Will you marry me?

He actually said that.

And I didn't know what to do, I froze.

And he almost seemed like he wanted to take it back. He shook his head and he wiped a hand across his face and he took a really deep breath. And I started to say something but he held a hand and stood up from the couch and looked out the window for a while with his back to me while I sat there having a goddamn heart attack. And I started to walk up to him but he told me no but I ignored him and I hugged him from behind and he relaxed and instead of turning to look into my eyes (which needed answers) he stood at the dirty glass attempting to count stars. And I couldn't find the heart to tell him not to look because it was useless, because the only star he ever needed was right here, skin on skin, and I would prove it if I had to.

Silence killed us for a while but he woke us up with a very quiet whisper of apology.

And I kissed his back and told him not to.

He said he shouldn't have gone that far but he was being honest and he was in love with me and he felt that it was the next step.

I asked him if he felt like if it was more of a leap than a step.

And he didn't answer right away because he knew it was a leap and I nuzzled into his back some more and told him that it was ok to be sorry because confusing leaps for steps was a common mistake that lovers made, and that I wasn't going to hold it against him because I would rather hold him.

And he bought it for a second but he tensed up and he turned to me and took me in his arms and made me look into his eyes and he was actually starting to tear up. I saw it in the moonlight. It was real. I never saw him like this before. It was like he was a new person. And I didn't know what to do. I grew scared because he was going over an edge that I knew was alright deep down, but on the surface, was frightening as hell.

We knew it was a moment but suddenly we both agreed it was time to go home. Sometimes these things happen. I got my stuff and he led me to my car and he opened the door. He started to say how sorry he was for ruining an awesome night but I kissed him to let him know it was ok. Because it was. It just caught me off guard. He didn't put up a fight. He shut the door and I put the keys in the ignition.

And then the phone rang.

bronwyn

Pick up pick up pick up pick up you silly little killer bitch, pick up pick up pick up, maybe I dialed the wrong number -

"Hello?"

"ELAINE."

"Bronwyn?"

"Yeah it's me, the ghost of your future holidays past. And you've just won a million dollars in the 'Crazy Drunk Bitch Sweepstakes.'"

Pause. Then: "What are you doing?"

"Nothing, why, what are you doing?"

"Um...talking to you..."

"Ok never mind that now. I find talking is tiring. Are you busy?"

"Um...right now?" She says it like she's in the middle of a goddamn physics exam or something.

"No, tomorrow, egghead, now." (I ALWAYS WANTED TO USE THAT LINE AND I AM SO HAPPY I FINALLY CAN.)

"Are you drunk?"

"Define drunk."

"You're drunk."

"I've only had a few waters."

"Jesus."

"Look look look, the drinking isn't important. Like, at all. Elaine. Please, tell me. What are you doing right now? Can you spare a few hours? It's important."

"A few hours?"

"Si. One hundred twenty minutes. Can you spare a movie length for your ol' pal, your ol' buddyroo?"

"What are you talking about?"

"Ok. I know. I'm being esoteric. Fine. But let's go be esoteric together."

"Ok, Bronwyn. Where are you calling me from and what are you doing?"

"Fine. What are you, my biographer? I'm in a bar parking lot and they kicked me out. But I was being wonderful and those fuckheads have no concept of what creativity, beauty, or free-thinking is, and the minute I opened my mouth and showed them I had a brain, well, they did the ol' switcheroo and here I sit with my ass on the dirt. In the dirt. I am the dirt, the dirt is me, there we go, we are infinite, full circle and feeling fine and open and having fun. Ok. What are you doing?"

I heard a very long pause on the other end, like she was coming up with an enormous lie, like she really voted for Romney instead of Obama, like she really hated Glee but watched it because her friends loved it and she wanted to fit in. "I'm just driving. I'm about to go home because I have work in the morning."

"You have sick days?"

"Why?"

"Ok. You do. So use one."

"Why?"

I gave a very heavy, sad sign on my end of the line. I wanted her to think I was depressed. Ok. I was. But I didn't want her to know that I was, I really wanted her to just THINK I was. Deception, I can do this, I'm a female. I can act with the best of them. Alright, maybe, just kinda stifle a sob. Disguise lighting a cigarette as a pained sob. Ok. And so I did. I made the exhale sound like I was getting ready to cry. And I choked briefly to make her think I was trying to be all macho and shit. And I think she fell for it. I felt bad for a second but then I remembered that I'm just a bad person and that it doesn't matter what I do because there is no hell, this is hell, because living in a world where Dimebag Darrell was murdered and George Michael is allowed to keep making shitty music, that to me is hell, and don't even bother arguing it or being whiny about it because I will punch the shit out of your soul.

"Is there something you need to say, Bronwyn? Are you safe?"

"Beware of safety," I said.

"What does that mean?"

"Ok, Elaine, I know you're confused. But I need to know something and you have to be honest with me because we're like superfriends now."

I don't think she got the reference. Which is a shame on her because if she needs to be in my life, she needs to appreciate the randomness of my diseased brain. A lot of people love it, so should she. We're like peas in a pod. "Ok. What is it?"

I took a really deep breath. Guilt and pain washed over me like I was in the ocean, like I was drowning and I had no limbs, no fight to fight the inevitable, the overwhelmingly powerful notion that this was all for something when it's really nothing. I thought of the younger me, the one on the bench, so blissfully unaware of all the damage. Finally I just decided that my drunk tongue would take over the conversation. There was no sense in pretending to be righteous or sober. So I said: "Where is your father buried?"

You'd think I punched her in the gut or rearranged her boy band CD's. "Why the fuck do you want to know?"

"Back the fuck up."

"No, Bronwyn. Why do you need to know?"

"Because. I need to know."

"Well, where's your father buried?"

I let it spill out before I could come up with a lie. I wanted to always have a story to give to people who asked (that didn't know already). But my anger came through. I wanted to destroy her because she was getting smart with me. Little did she know, I was her fucking savior. And she needed to respect that shit right quick. So I tuned it up a little bit. She hasn't seen the real Bronwyn. I'll make that incident in church look like a tea party. So I turned up the accent. I channeled my dad. And it worked. "If you need to know, Elaine, I'm going to fucking tell you. We cremated his Mick ass. We put him in a fucking oven like a fucking pizza and burnt him into a crisp and we put him into a urn in case people GAVE A SHIT and no one did so we took the ashes, no actually, I took the ashes because Mom was too drunk to care, so I took the ashes with me and I put them in a plastic bag and I went and bought his favorite beer which was Guinness if you need to know fucking gag me right and I drank that shit down as fast as I could and then I put his ashes in every beer bottle all twenty-four of them, I made sure they were all even, and I put into the fucking landfill and watched it go. That's where my dad is. I mean, I guess I have no idea where he is. I never read the obituary. I never saw his side again. Ever. They're all fucking sheep in Ulster for all I care. SO UNLESS YOU HAVE SOMETHING A LITTLE MORE DEPRESSING you have to tell me where he is because I'm only trying to help your ass. That's all

I'm trying to do. God damn it. Elaine, I'm trying to make your life BETTER. If you don't think I am, then hang up the phone and we'll forget all about each other. Jesus. Fuck. I know you think I'm this weirdo. But I have more heart than half the fuckers you know. I want. I need. I feel. I bleed. I just do. And I'm so honest. I'm so goddamn honest I could puke. So there. Ashes. He's ashes. What else? Where is he? Is he at least in a coffin? Did he have a respectable final end? Did the curtain close properly, or did it get stuck, like most curtains often do?" I felt blood again. I lit two cigarettes at once again. I became death, the destroyer of worlds, briefly. And I hated it. But then at the same time, I felt cleansed. Like I was a new set of bones, a new prototype of unstretched, soft skin and an untainted mind, ready for the world. And I waited for what she could possibly even say to that. Because I know it wouldn't match what I said. I felt really powerful. But it wouldn't last long. Empires crumble way too easily, like they're made of rotted wood or reject metals or any other organic material that some hippy-dippy tree-hugger would find completely acceptable. And I sat smoking, drunk, unwanted in any home ever, in the history of any town of anywhere.

And she responded after a long while. I hit her with a bomb, I know this. And she wasn't expecting it. I thought she would have hung up the phone. But she didn't. She hung on. And it was with tears probably that she answered: "In Pottsgrove."

"Where?"

"Lower."

"In what graveyard?"

"St. Aloysius."

"I know where that is. Meet me there."

"Why?" Her voice grew cold and bitter, like she was ready to die or explode.

"Because I need you to."

"No. It's late."

"What does that have to do with anything?"

"You can't go that late. It's trespassing. It's the rules."

"Fuck the rules."

"God made those rules."

"I don't care who made it."

"Excuse me?"

"You heard me."

"No, I don't think I did. What did you say?"

"I SAID WHO GIVES A SHIT. I'm trying to help."

"You keep saying that, Bronwyn. But I don't know how. Maybe if you wouldn't talk like you own the whole goddamn world and everybody in it."

"Well maybe if you took the stick out of your ass you'd be able to see what I'm doing. Judging by the little tone that your voice has decided to take, I can tell that you rarely go see him or even drop by or even think about where he's buried. It's a thing called respect. And if you want to get over this, if you want to get better - "

"I never said I wasn't - "

" - then get in your little POS and meet me there."

"Don't you tell me what to do."

"Well, who else will? You seem like you just run around and do what you want anyway."

"I'm NOT meeting you there at NIGHT. That's trespassing."

"On who? THE DEAD? They don't care. In fact, they're probably glad we're COMING."

"That's God's territory."

"It's the townships. You think angels cut the lawn? No. They pay someone minimum wage. It's got nothing to do with miracles or wings or penance. Come on, Elaine. Seriously."

"You're such a fucking bitch."

"Yes, yes, I am. And you're delaying your own progress."

There was a pause. Did I finally hit her hard enough? During the silence, I reached into my glove compartment to make sure my little dinky switchblade was still in there. Sure enough. I always make sure there's something to defend myself with. This will have to do, if Elaine decides to want to have my face for dinner later. If she ever gets up the courage to do the right thing, to respect the dead, to move on and not be such a whore about everything. I grabbed the knife and I let it sit in my hand as I waited for her on the other line. I watched cars dance by. I watched the bar lights live on without me. In my complete fit of rage, I realize that by kicking me out, I never paid them for anything I drank.

I started laughing.

"What's your problem now?" I heard her say.

"I beat the system," I whispered.

"What system?"

"White America," I said.

"You're deranged," she said.

"Tell me something I don't know," I said.

"Alright, I'll tell you something that I think you don't know," she said, and it sounded like she was alone, so she suddenly raised her voice to a sheer, reckoning trill. "I think you're the type of person who's so afraid that they can barely stand. I think you're so fucking full of shit about everything. I think you make it all up just so you can be liked, so you can fit in with people. Your dad isn't dead. He's alive and well. You're just playing an act, writing a story, trying to make something out of yourself when there's clearly nothing there at all. Your dad was no drunk. Your dad loves your mom and they're sitting at home right now, wondering what they did to give birth such a fucked up girl."

I was blown away a bit, I had to admit. It was a cold calculated attempt to piss me off. And it was slowly working. And I was losing my grip on her, so I had to get it back somehow. It's a shame that this was starting to turn into a game instead of a friendship, which is what I really intended it to be.

But if she really hated me, she wouldn't have been talking to me for this long, telling me how horrible I was. So secretly, she was waiting for me to redeem myself, so she could justify everything, because she needs me as much as I need her. It's awful how people do this to themselves. They use themselves to the point where they're not useful. And what have you done then? Mastered the art of being an asshole?

"So my dad's alive, eh?"

"Yeah, I think so. He's waiting for you to come home."

"Is he?"

"Yes."

"So we can have family dinner?"

"That's right."

"And he can ask me about how school is going and how work is going?"

"All of those things."

"And then I can hear all about his day and watch Mom and him smile longingly at each other and they secretly play footsies because they're still in love?"

There was a pause. Then a "Yeah."

"Yeah. That'll be waiting for me when I get home. And then after dinner we'll sit at the table and talk about the future?"

"That's usually what happens."

"And then I can watch him grow older and have increasing amounts of respect and think to myself, 'this will never leave me'".

Another pause. Then: "Yes."

"Elaine."

There was crying. I had made her think of all of those memories. All of those faint glimpse of time, rolled into one ball of guilt. I made her eat her words. I didn't want to, because I know she wasn't hungry. But I had to. It was the only way to win. She sat there thinking of all of it and I knew I was such a horrible person, even in my drunk state. I started to take my camera out of my bag and I got out of the car and I stood behind it and I took a photo of my car looking out onto the dark road and the night. I needed to get this down. I waited for her on the phone. I didn't pressure. Finally I heard:

"Bronwyn."

"Yes?"

"I'll meet you there."

"Sounds good."

"I'll be there as soon as I can."

"I will, too," I said. And I hung up the phone. And I stood there and I took a few more pictures of the world. It just felt like the thing to do.

elaine

My dad's funeral was on a Wednesday night. It rained. Not even that. It poured. And it was cold, even for spring. We all came in black and everyone's suit or blouse was wrinkled and old, not fitting right and full of cat hair. I was nauseous. We had reservations at a shitty steakhouse afterwards and no one wanted to go. But we did. We dressed in our best and we straightened collars and we all stuffed tissues in our pockets and deeply sighed and attempted to look for something new in the sky but failed miserably. The rain fell on our clothes. We were cold. We just wanted to go to sleep. It was only the middle of the week and we still had two days before we could rest, or even try to rest. No one wanted to work. The funeral director was a quiet old man who didn't care who we were because he does this all the time, and that he didn't give two shits about Dad because he just saw it as another stiff adding to his bank account, his watches, his suits, his shoes, his big-ass car. His name was Jeremiah. He had horrible glasses. His skin felt like sandpaper. Mom did not want to shake his hand. We both wore pearls; who the hell knows why. The rain meant umbrellas and we all had to throw them into the same copper bin up front, wet, unfolded, and I think someone stole my blue one, which I had since I was seven, and it wasn't really important, but on that day, I remember thinking, *really? How fucked are these people?* We went in before everyone else just to make sure Dad looked ok. Mom lost it. I just looked at his face. Jeremiah had done a horrible job. Everything about that guy was just horrible. His breath, his countenance, his thoughts. He probably tried to grope every female cousin and friend I had with a double handshake or a half-attempt hug, sneaky-like. But messing with Dad's face was the worst. He tried to duplicate a devil may care grin because Mom told him at our first meeting that he always had a smile on his face. And this idiot thought that happiness translated into some form of deceitful charm, and I never remember him smiling like that. And I remember wanting to leave right fucking there because nothing was right. It was all going to hell so fast. I looked out through the dirty windows that probably haven't cleaned in months and all I saw was rain and I remember thinking that Dad was going to get so wet when we put him into the ground. We couldn't even get one moment of sunshine for a man who provided so much sunlight for us. It was all bullshit. But Mom kept putting her hand on my shoulder trying to calm me down. But what was the point of that? It's not like that was going to make this funeral any better. And I remember after all of the greetings that it looked like they were dimming the house lights just to be dramatic and angelic and all that. And I remember saying something to a friend of mine that it was all bullshit and Mom overheard that comment and she led me to the side and told me to be more lady-like. And I told her that how can you stand there and let them do this to Dad, because this is not how he looked, this is not how he was. And her face contorted into her own little strange sad smile and she just hugged me and told me how pretty I was. And more and more people flooded into a dim-lit room and I wanted to yell but there was soft music playing now and my heart just wanted to jump out of my chest, spread out all over their shitty, ugly rug. Time went and bled all over itself, making a fool of us all. It amazes me, the will of instinct, I remember thinking again as I watched clocks and shook hands. That's the problem, I always remember, always always always remember the goddamn dumb stuff, except what I needed to forget, which was ALL OF THIS.

And then we went to the graveyard. And everyone's sitting in the rain sobbing and I remember sitting up front underneath the small tent they put off so the coffin didn't get soaked, like that even mattered now because they did so much to screw him up. And everyone else was getting wet probably because their umbrellas were stolen by some funeral home worker, like that's some great Christian thing to do. And the pastor (the same pastor I told off) started his spiel and promised that all of this rain and cold was God's way of giving us a beautiful last moment of a great man's life and I snorted pretty loudly because this was God's terrific plan and humanity be damned and Mom didn't catch it but my one cousin did and she gave me a little push out of anger. And I remember thinking that she didn't understand, and ever since that moment, we haven't been getting on very well. Because why would God give us some crappy day like this if this was supposed to be gorgeous and golden and perfect? And we had argued about that afterwards, me and her at home, about how she was just a close-minded bitch who only saw solace in her clothes instead of reality and she screamed back at me saying that she was glad that Dad was dead which was bullshit because he was her uncle so he was A PART OF HER and she wept like a little baby too so she was just as guilty and fucked as me. But anyway, the pastor went on his manifesto until I stood up and told him that I couldn't take his condescending "message" anymore and to hurry up and just put him in the grave so we could eat the caterer's food already. That was the moment that won me the never-ending wrestling match with the therapists. Which I didn't deserve but nonetheless I do not remember most of that night. I remember crying. I remember my stomach hurting and the world ending and the softest poetry I could ever conceive turn rock solid and ugly, turn black and burnt and twisted in a matter of seconds, and I with no hands, I with no feet, could do nothing to right the ship of which reality and fantasy collided, where dream and nightmare fell forward and died its death, wanting blood back in its brain in order to give me perfect reason to fight and claw and scratch again.

All of that flooded back when I pulled into the graveyard where these sullen beautiful souls slept in a limitless, music less cold. Her car and mine were the only ones here. No one came here late because they weren't supposed to because they had respect, unlike us two, who were desecrating something meaningful. And of course, like an idiot (even though I didn't expect her to know where my father's grave was), she was parked in a section nowhere near the right grave, looking at headstones with a flashlight and singing some shitty song at the top of her lungs. One of her punk rock anthems that had no legs or foundation to be loved.

I rolled my window down and shouted. "SHUT UP."

She whirled around and nearly fell in the mud and raised her flashlight at me like a cop. She saw me and she waved. Then she stumbled again. I drove my car right up to hers and got out with the lights still on and the engine running and I ran up to her and pulled her out of the dirty grass and she pushed me away.

"Some things I can do myself, ya know," she said. "I assure you, Officer, I've only had a few ales."

"You just love being a mess, don't you?"

"Oh, I don't see you sitting high and mighty either," she said. "Your shit stinks just like mine. Maybe even worse."

I try to think of an angry response but can't think of anything so I walk back to my car and shut it off. It's just us and the crickets and the stars and the dead. It's almost beautiful, surprisingly enough. But I can't think straight to give her gratification or assurance, so I walk back with fists made, ready to pummel, but probably will be beaten right back. Because Bronwyn has a deadly insight that I do not care for or admire but unfortunately respect. I see her sitting in front of a grave and she shines the light at me and through the blinding beam I see her bloodshot eyes. Everything about her was blood. Physically, mentally. It was exhausting.

"Self preservation," she whispers to me.

"What does that mean?"

"It means," she said as she put the flashlight down and pulled at grass that didn't need to be in her hands, "that you keep yourself the way you want, get rid of the stuff you want, be the stuff you want to be, and ignore the stuff that people want you to be, all in one swift move."

"And how does one do that?"

"Get drunk," she sniffed, "and confront your fears."

"I don't drink."

She reached behind her and there was her bag, at the ready, full of destruction. Sure enough, she pulls out a small bottle of what looks like vodka. Clear, dangerous, smells like crap. She opens the cap with her teeth somehow and she hands it to me.

"You're fucked, Bronwyn."

"Your dad," she tells me, "would want this."

And I smacked the bottle out of her hand. It fell to the ground with a soft noise, and some spilled out, but Bronwyn caught it from spilling more, stood it up, and took the small puddle that did spill into a handmade cup and brought it to her lips. Drank it all down.

"You don't tell me what my father would WANT."

"Jesus made wine," she tells me, "and you make excuses."

"And what do you make?"

"Reasoning," she says.

I'm ready to murder her. "You are so fucked. You have no idea."

"Oh, I do. Trust me. Ol' Pops drilled that into my head," she said. "And now it's time you be the same. You need to be the fear. You need to be all of it."

I could only stare at her. I left my phone at the car. I wish I had it with me in case of emergency. Pretty soon someone would drive by and see us here and call the police and I did not want that on my record. She probably didn't care. She probably had a million arrests by now.

"Ok, Elaine," she said, standing up with the bottle in her hand and drinking, "you don't want to do this the easy way. Fine. But. You need just to accept something."

"What's that?" I said, crossing my arms, shivering a little, either from the weather or from her just being here.

"Your dad doesn't give a shit about who you are now or what you'll be."

I didn't know what to say. Was she even right?

"He's only concerned about you, as a thing. As an entity. He died knowing you were going to live somehow. He didn't give a shit about what you're going to do with your life because all he knew was that you wanted life so bad that you would cheat death for as long as you could. And that was enough for him. He doesn't care if you're going to be a doctor or a lawyer. He just wants you to live because HE COULDN'T. Get it yet?"

I let some time go before I said, "Are you saying that's what he thought before he went?"

"It's possible."

"He was DRIVING. He wasn't THINKING anything. He was just being."

"Isn't that the same? Just being? Isn't just being thinking idle thoughts? Do you think he cared about your motives for doing what you did that day? Or do you think he was going through the motions because he was so USED to it?"

I stared at her. She drank from the bottle and swayed. "Fuck, Elaine. Show me his real grave. I don't even know who this guy is."

We walked in tense silence until we got to the right one. Fourth row, sixth one in. We stood there for a minute as I took it all in. It was still so weird to see his name carved into the pink marble. I thought of all the things I could have done to be a better daughter. I looked over at Bronwyn briefly. She almost seemed transfixed. At least that's what it looked like in the hard night sky. Like she was praying. Like she was normal, like she was respecting something finally other than her completely fucked values. She even put the vodka to the side as we both stood there, cold, looking at this stone that just didn't seem right. I sighed and started to tear up a bit. Bronwyn suddenly knelt down to it and started to do something I couldn't see right away.

"What are you doing?"

She didn't answer.

I said it louder.

She said, "There's bird shit on here. I'm trying to get it off."

I said, "Leave it alone."

"I'm trying to - "

"Just leave it alone!" I said sharply.

"Why?"

I pulled her away. She fell on her ass and looked up at me. "Elaine, I was trying to clean your father's fucking HEADSTONE."

"I DIDN'T ASK YOU TO," I said.

She got on her feet. She had a drink from her vodka. I wanted to break her arms.

"What is it exactly do you want?"

"I want him back," I said, pointing at the stone, "and I don't want you fucking it up."

She shook her head. "You never really listening to a fucking word I said, didn't you?"

"Why should I?"

"Drink." She thrust the bottle into my direction.

"No."

"Please."

"Bronwyn."

"Please?"

"Why?"

"I want you to be my friend, god fucking damnit. Why do you have to question everything? Seriously, Elaine, everything?" And she put the bottle into my direction again. Insisting. Being a pest.

"I don't see what that has to do with my father," I said coldly.

She stood there under stars offering me the alcohol. So I finally took it. And I kept my eyes on her and I brought it to my lips and I took a swig and I coughed like a bastard. She laughed. Of course she would. It was her nature. I tried to hand it back to her but she waved me off and she pissed me off so I took another drink and it burned just the same. I coughed some more and thought I would throw up and thought about how Mom would disapprove so I tried to hand it back and she waved me off and mouthed the words "one more" so I did and somehow the burning seemed a little less prevalent so I kept the bottle in my hand and felt the glass and somehow the stars and the crickets made sense despite my anger and my ambivalence on being here and her seeing where my dead father slept.

"How do you feel?" She asked me.

"Like shit," I said.

"Good."

"Why is that good?"

"Because it means you feel something. Other than normal. Normal is not good. But shit? That I can accept," she said to me as she looked out into the black horizon. The same houses I always looked at, the same people I always wondered about. "Shit makes you think how you got there. Normal just makes you happy that you're just SOMEWHERE."

"How did you learn to be like this?" I asked her. "You don't even sound right when you talk. Like you're not even with it. Like you're far off in some place where no one even wants you there. Like you're above all else and not even wanting to be with the people you have to be with."

"I'm here with you, aren't I?"

"I guess."

"Ok. Then it's choice. That's all it is. Like you had a choice to do what you're doing now.

Honey, it takes two to tango. So don't act like you're the paragon of moral virtue."

I chuckled.

"What do you feel right now about your dad?"

"Are you my therapist?"

"I am now. Drink."

"No."

"So tell me about your dad. What could you say to him right now if he just rose up out of here and showed up and stood here? Not like a zombie dad, but you know, like how he was."

I waited for a very long time and I'm sure Bronwyn understood it as love but I was afraid she would interpret it as something else because she is known for that. I stood there with one hand in my pocket and the other on her vodka bottle, trying to stand up straight, trying to appear like I wasn't going to lose my shit. It was very hard to face this after all, I realize. You go through life assuming. You go through your life sleeping and waiting at red lights, all waiting for something to come along. But instead you wind up stopping. And looking at obstacles. And hating them for a while, but then coming to appreciate them for what they are. And they're not even obstacles, after a while, or roadblocks even. They're people, too, in a way. And will people ever know that besides me? Will they know they can love as me?

bronwyn

I stood there waiting, thinking, my God, does it take you this long to think every thought ever? Just talk. Open your mouth and speak. I'm not going to judge you. I do that every second of every day anyway. You ain't gonna change my mind, dear. And I went to get the bottle of vodka out of her little trembling hand and she pulled it closer to herself suddenly so I backed off. She was transforming slightly. I wasn't sure whether it was good or bad so I gave her a brief moment of privacy and I looked at my phone and nothing there and so I looked off into the stars and tried to count the lights still left on in all these houses and wondered when the cops would come to tell us we were being menaces to society. If they knew what was good for them, they would just keep driving right by, not concerning themselves with such grieving young geniuses. We're all just waiting for our moment to shine. And that moment will not come until we are both losing our minds.

Just to get a rise out of her, I decide to light a cigarette, but she doesn't even say a word. So I smoke like a madman. I blow the smoke into the wind in hoping I can give some to the dead, and finally, she brings another drink to her lips, and says to me, "I think I've been wrong about love my whole life and it hurts to say that so don't even respond to it. I'm just thinking out loud. I've been wrong about love."

I nod and keep smoking. She's getting there. She's slowly seeing what it's like to practice the fine art of LETTING SHIT GO.

"I don't think Dad would even care about what I would want to be. I think as long as I don't go the way that he went, that he would be fine with whatever I did. And life isn't about what you grow up to be, as long as you grow up into something." She suddenly sits down in the grass, clutching the bottle. I remain standing. "I've tried so hard to be okay with all of this. But I fear that I've made some mistakes along the way. I spin stories. Sometimes I don't get all the details right. And I think it's either grief or karma or some other petty bullshit. It's probably God getting back at me. Heh." And then she starts laughing for some reason and I just keep smoking until she looks at me with wet, disturbed eyes.

"What stories have you spun to me?" I ask her finally, probably so she can confess and move on.

"I can't think of any right now," she mumbles.

"What about that one with the fight in the locker room?"

She thinks for a moment and turns away from me and looks at the headstone and says, "No, that was all completely true." I nod. I believe her. Finally I decide to sit down next her for a while, nothing else to do. She's starting to turn. I'm proud of her. I nudge her and she looks at me and I motion that I want a drink and she hands me the bottle, although with a little bit of a sadness. This must be her first time drinking. Which depresses me. How do you go through this life and live in this America and not drink? Sometimes people are just way too crazy for me.

"Elaine, what I've been trying to do, I think you need to know that - "

"It was done under love," she cuts in. "It was done under a love that has been redefined by two people who have lost the concept of love, that the misconception that they will always be loved by something subsequent and whole has now gave way to some artificial type of love made by people who need to create something out of ashes and bullshit and misplaced things. So dreams and all that are bonded with other things to make love. And that's the type of love that its tough because it does not go into you fully. It's forcing a square peg into a round hole. You push until someone finally accepts." And she punches the ground and starts to cry.

I can't say I would disagree with her assessment. I take a healthy dose of the vodka. It goes down really nice although I guess I really should stop drinking since she's underage and we're both driving and we're kinda trespassing. But who cares? It's beautiful. It's an amazing feeling to say fuck the rules, and if you want to live your life by what the police say, go right ahead, be boring, don't have any original thoughts. I'll be on the edge, thank you very much. She punches the ground a few more times and I hold my hand out so she stops and calms down and she does. She looks straight into the headstone for a few more minutes.

"I promised him, at the funeral, that I would never drink a day in my life," she says and turns to me. There's a fire growing. "Because of how he died. And now look at me. I'm that person. Just like that. Now what?"

"I don't think it's exactly like that."

"Why isn't it?"

"Because you would never - " And I want to say she would never kill anybody although she has now said that to me before, face to face, and I try to think of the right way to say what I want to say because she is close to cracking, close to being a new person, and I have to be careful with the fragile pieces because I want big pieces, not fragmented useless things.

"Do you want to know where I used to go when I couldn't take it anymore?"

She turns her head away from me, starts to pick at her fingers. She sighs once and goes to start another monologue but she can't get the words out so she just gives up and looks ahead into nothing. I sit on the neighboring headstone and she doesn't complain so I talk.

"I made up a world where nothing has no name, where it is all beauty constantly. There are rivers and there's sky and there's homes where men and women and children are all doing things that they want. And none of it has any name. It's just a place. It's where I can imagine a river just being a river and nothing else. And sky just being sky and nothing else. And it's dumb, I know, in fact, it actually sounds really fucking retarded. But it helped me remember that I'm not the only one here that has this problem. In this world, we're all together. And no one's fighting. No one has any war in their head. It's all peace." She's not buying it. "Ok, Elaine, I know I'm an asshole. I act like one, I look like one, I did some...really rotten things to you in the last couple of days and I barely know you. I get that. And I know what you're saying. She's so full of SHIT. She sits there and she talks about some dumb little fantasy world and all Bronwyn is...well, she's just a cunt. And I am a cunt. But I know what it's like to hurt. It's been like this for years, honey. And you, you're just getting started. But what I'm trying to say to you now

212

is that you have a chance to come up with your own little world, whatever, whichever, however you want to play it. There are no rules. Just call the shots the way you want it. The way you see it, go for it. You don't agree with God, you don't like God? Fuck it, baby. BE GOD."

And then I hand her the bottle back.

And she takes it and downs it completely.

This may or may not be totally good, but I'm willing to give it a chance.

She's fine for the first couple of seconds, but then she starts to dry heave, and then she's looking ready to puke, so I gently step down from the headstone and she's gagging so I quick untie her hair from her ponytail and hold it back and I coax her softly until she hacks and hems and haws and finally she upchucks all over the headstone. And it's definitely not a pretty one (not like any of them ever are, but this one kinda looked like a rainbow) and her dad's name is obscured and she starts to cry and cough and I whisper that it's ok. I reach into my bag and I give her a bottle of water and I start to take off my hoodie and I start to wipe the puke off the marble slab as she drinks and drinks to regain her intended, beloved normalcy. I do feel bad. I didn't mean to make her sick. I just tried to be a good friend. And she's trying to stop me from using my clothes to clean it up but I just tell her to drink and she does and I get all of it off and it's a sickening stench, like she had been eating onions or hummus or some disgusting vegan shit or something. I gingerly grab the hoodie by the actual hood and I walk it over to a nearby green garbage can and drop it in unceremoniously. The cold didn't bother me. I have ice water in my veins already - at least that's what my Mom said. And I go back to Elaine but she's talking now under her breath, and I know exactly what she's doing. She's asking for forgiveness. It'll be the last time she does so, because I remember my last time asking my dead sack of shit father for penance, and he didn't exactly give it to me. I remember not ever wanting to do it again, but it doesn't hurt to try. I give her a few minutes. I hum a few bars of "Young Man Blues" and remind myself that I need to buy *Fever Hunting* because I would never download an album of theirs. I'm a purist. I go back to looking at her.

She's crying, practically hugging the stone. It's embarrassing but it's an important step to healing so I let her go. She's saying she's sorry. I look around. Maybe it's time to go. She may be unprepared for what's going to happen next to her.

I walk up to her. Before I could even open my mouth, she turns to me and she's full of rage and anger and self-pity. Her voice takes on a new volume.

"Teach me about death," she says.

"What?"

"You think you're so goddamn smart. You want to talk about life? Talk to me about death. I need to know about death."

"What death? Elaine..."

"You went through it. Didn't the old you have to die in order to become a new you? Isn't the old Bronwyn dead somewhere? Isn't this the newly created, freshly started Bronwyn that you are now? Didn't a lot of you die to become the person you want?"

More than you will ever know, I thought. I said nothing.

"Well, I need to know about death."

"No, Elaine. That's not what this is about. This is about life."

"Fuck you. You know. Tell me."

"Don't talk to me like that. I just wiped your fucking VOMIT off your father's HEADSTONE."

"Bronwyn, please."

"Jesus, Elaine. You can't talk like that. That's not what all this was about. It's not about dying. It's just about starting over. You got it all wrong."

"No, I don't. I just can't let things go like you apparently can't. You're so different. I admire it, in a way. You can just say 'fuck it' and move on."

"It wasn't always like that. You think it's all fucking roses and doilies. It ain't."

"You got into my life. I didn't ask you to. And now you're not going to just walk away. I need to know what you know. You're so smart."

"No, I'm not. I'm fucking stupid."

"Stop that."

"Elaine, it's time to go home. Come on. I'll follow behind you so you don't get pulled over."

"Oh, no, you're not getting off that easily."

"Are you threatening me again? Because if you are, I'm not going to let you get away with it. I am not afraid of you, Elaine."

"Well, you really should be." And she finally stood up, covered in dirt, red-eyed, half drunk, half insane, a hybrid of monster and person. I guess it was time she finally wanted to prove to me she was worth a fight, that she wasn't all books and bullshit and bandages.

"Don't act like a tough bitch now just because you're drunk."

"Bronwyn."

"What?"

"Don't test me."

"I'll do as I goddamn please. Get in the car. It's time to go home."

"You don't know my dad like I did," she said.

"I know this, duh," I say, throwing my arms wide. "Jesus. I wanted you to look into yourself. Not go psycho."

"I did. And I want to know about death."

"Stop it."

"I'M NOT GOING TO STOP IT!" She screamed.

I looked around to see if any more house lights would pop on. If we weren't doing enough to get us in trouble. All the community needed was two drunk idiots yelping and yawping at the top of their lungs about petty crap.

"Lower your voice," I said, pointing a finger at her.

"Don't you point at me," she said, snarling. Apparently she was ready to show me her claws. She looked crazed. She looked like she had never seen semblance in her life.

"Elaine, if you're going to do something, you better do it now. Because I don't want to hurt you. I will if I have to."

"You don't know about hurt."

"The fuck I don't."

"You don't know what it's like."

She's drunk. She's slurring. She never felt this way in her entire sheltered life, in all her numbered days. I tried to find the right way to handle this. I put a hand on her shoulder. It was a gigantic mistake. She shrugged it off violently. I put it back on her shoulder and she did the same thing. I saw the look in her eyes. She wanted to come at me. So I prepared myself. I let myself get ready. I held up two fucked up fists, shaking, ready to bleed for any cause, anytime, anywhere. I would die if I had to. I almost want to tell her, don't kill me. I'm trying to do good for the world. I take pictures. And your whole life,

Elaine, it's just a picture, it's just card stock in my binder. Please understand that.

"You don't tell me I don't know what hurt is. My father beat me," I tell her. A little lie doesn't hurt. It doesn't help. But it doesn't hurt.

"Bullshit."

I pull my shirt down so she can see a bruise around my neck that I gave myself. It's dark out and it's drunk so she won't remember specifics. "See that? That's a present. Non-fucking-returnable, Elaine. So now what? Are we playing cards? What's your hand? If you're going to fuck me up, just do it."

And she did surprisingly.

She charged me and caught me off guard.

She tore into the skin around my eyes and she tugged, trying to take my eyelids and I almost thought for a second she bit, baring her perfect white suburban teeth, but I lifted my knee into her fucking groin and she howled for a minute and she gave away, and I took the moment to roll over and I decided the best course of action would be to choke her, and clumps of mud fell out of my hair into her mouth onto her tongue, and even though the dirt entered her throat all she kept screaming was "I wish

I never met you, I wish he never died" and all I could say was "I wish he didn't die, I wish he was still alive so I would never know you" and neither of us could gain proper advantage until she managed to hit me in the stomach and it got me in the right spot and I tried to get back to my feet but she was off me and she was holding the (now) empty bottle of vodka. I stared at her and she broke the glass over her father's headstone and a large shard lay in her palm and she was going to stab me with it, I was sure of it. But instead she cut a decent-sized scar into her arm and she held it in for a while and I tried to stop her but I couldn't and even in the dark I saw the blood and then she dropped the shard and took a good long look at me and whispered even though she didn't have to.

"Your blood and my blood," she said, "right here, finally." And she just left me standing there, confused as fuck. She got into her car. I couldn't even stop her. She seemed almost possessed. She drove off, swerving a little bit, but she got onto the road like a champ and just kept going, never stopping, even for a minute, to consider how I was.

I was lost. I just sat there for a while, looking at her father's grave, trying to feel the emotion. What the fuck just happened? Did I just lose control of someone? Did I just lose control of MYSELF?

I smoked a cigarette.

elaine

Hey child, you're not safe here.

There is no such thing as meridian, there is no such thing as kingdom come.

And my eyes can no longer contain the good things I keep with me to take as means of love to protect myself from means of evil.

These pastors and therapists and punks. There is no wall of which keeps them out. My pulse goes haywire. The love is sinking down into a bottomless pool, no reprieve, not one form of apology, not one inkling of sorrow for the pretty girl born with this - a life of death, a fatherless daughter, and not one shit given for what she will eat or drink tomorrow, no, there is only pats on the back and prayers meant to be said seventeen times while you soak yourself in your tears, left with shoes that don't fit to walk on empty, cold streets.

Oh, he speaks to me, and I'm not talking about God anymore. But it isn't the same. He talks and it fades like everything is meant to. It is coherent enough but it is not meant to survive because our atmospheres are just too different, too much in separation - it does not get translated well enough. It dies.

I miss him but he does not miss me because he said goodbye already. Once you do that, it doesn't matter. Saying goodbye is slamming the door. Infinity, there's the music, that noise, that fits with it so well.

I do not miss you, Elaine, truth be told, no splitting hairs or dodging bullets. It is not relative nor speculative. It is what it is. Elaine, there is no reason to be sad over this pile of bones. Why hang on? Let go. Rest your fingers. Your mother will be fine. She's learned to be a warrior in her spare time over the years. I went quick. Not a lot of pain. Some.

But nothing that will keep me up at night. Nor should it keep you up either.

And then it hits me as I'm driving and I must pull over again for the third time. I must. A blur settles in, confines me. I am simply not well.

I puke in my lap.

I'm drunk and Dad is talking to me.

There must be a better way to live this life other than Bronwyn's way.

And I have to find it way and make it work for me.

I'm looking at the stars and they're all bullshit, once again. Everything they told you when you were younger, now you finally see when you grow, how all of it was just to make you stupid and to hold you back from discovering how machines REALLY work.

The trick is that they don't.

You only think they do.

Cages with cheap bars, houses with laughing walls.

Dad's body, young, in pieces.

The thought of death keeps rolling around in my head, mixing. I'm almost enamored with the fact that it chose my father. Just so I could learn more faster. So I could be privileged unlike all my friends, to have a secret wealth of beautiful knowledge. And I wish to tell them all if I ever get out of this hole that I'm in, that it's not so bad. Maybe everyone should go through it. So we all could learn, co-exist, be beautiful damaged things and have pasted-on wings and fly into the sun and moon together.

I don't think I like being drunk. Or maybe I do. And I'm morphing into one of Bronwyn's little playthings. How many other people has she changed?

My phone is ringing.

And it's her.

I look at it like it's a ghost. Because it is.

But I let it go. The same old ringtone that I can't change because I'm so used to it, it's beaten in me. It goes to voicemail. I don't even want to talk. I physically can't. All of what is running through my head wouldn't be prim and proper to tell another living soul. I just let it run fluid. Maybe it will mature with age.

I throw the phone in the glove compartment. Let it play for the manual. Let it play for the title and registration. I am not in the mood for her music or her words. I have too many things to figure out. Where am I going to go? What am I going to do? Am I just going to go home and watch a movie and try to sleep and then just wake up and go to work? Like nothing happened? Fuck. That.

I refuse to go back to the graveyard. I could never. I attacked her. Like I said I would. And that part, I don't even know. Should I be proud of that? Was I defending his honor or mine? What was I even thinking, agreeing to come out? What was I doing drinking?

And out of anger, I head butt the steering wheel twice. Until I stop and realize what I'm doing. I'm just like her.

Just. Like. Her.

And I didn't draw blood but it's obvious what I did because it's slightly bruised. Maybe I can pass it off as something else. Fatigue. A nightmare come alive, seeping from my thoughts through my skin. There's no leaving now. There's just being.

I hate that she may be right.

I can't live with that thought.

I'm watching all these cars aimlessly mill about, looking for warmth and companionship.

Looking for the next trip, the long road, the engine's constant beating. It has everything it needs to go on. Unlike me and a million others.

The phone is ringing again.

I know it's her and I'm not going to even check. It's pointless.

I get back on the road and try to get home without being pulled over. It's easier than you think. In fact, it's probably one of the most easiest things I had to do so far.

bronwyn

Mistakes are easy to make. They're our favorite thing to do. That's why we do them all the time. We love being fuck ups. And of course you don't ever want to be one, but you are every day of your life. You just are. Don't act like you never feel that way or think you're one of those people who are perfect. Because you aren't. You just fuck up maybe a little less. But you're not special. I thought I would be one of those people that would always avoid it. Look how that one turned out. I am not so lucky after all. And I sit here wondering if I did the right thing with Elaine or not, but deep down, I know that I did in a way and that in an even bigger way, I did not. It was a dream that I had years ago when my old man finally kicked the bucket. That was I going to be a counselor. And instead I was hell bent on destroying myself because that was the cheaper option of the two. I didn't have the money to spend to be all wonderful and to have a career. So I just went with my gut, which just said, kill. So I did. Little by little, these cells of mine don't have the energy to make more, and whatever I have left is whatever I have left. I think I can live with that. Good thing I don't have to live with it forever. That would be a terrible burden, to grow old and be wonderful and to have helped people your entire life.

And in these last few days I know that Elaine was something that I could not handle. It was a mistake thinking she was a proper person. It was a mistake fighting with her, with talking to her. All of it was just a gigantic mistake. And I wanted to right it because I don't think I can live with the fact that she has the upper hand now. All my life, I swore that I wouldn't let someone think they're better than me, even if they were, and even if it meant getting killed over it. No one is supposed to have those thoughts, and if they do, they are not meant to be carried out or last very long. They're just errant little problems, meant to be erased quickly and forgotten about soon after. But when someone thinks it, really BELIEVES it, really makes it their modus operandi, then there's a situation that Bronwyn cannot live with. That's why I kicked Dad in the head. He thought he was better than me. That's why I drink. Because my liver thinks it's better than me. And that's why I think that Elaine would be better off knowing about death, because she thinks that she's better than me. And I'm not sitting here saying that I'm going to do anything about her. No. I don't do that to people. I don't KILL people. I just think that I'm going to lead her in the right direction if that she wants so bad, and I think it's noble. That's what she wants so bad, right? I heard her say it again and again. Death, death. That's what she wants to know about, well then, I can make that happen. It'll make her regret thinking that she was going to beat me in a battle of wits.

Ugh. Listen to myself.

I don't want to be a person like that. Pops did that, all the time. He'd get drunk and rant about wanting to hurt perfectly innocent people. Maybe some were innocent, with him who never knows, but he was bold enough to boast that he could beat up anybody, that he was a boxer back in his day, that he would have no problem showing someone that he meant business. And half the time when he said that crap, you just played it off as him being insane. But there were times when he whispered it, where he didn't get angry and manly about it, where it was a calm kind of temper, where he said it quietly enough so that you believed him, so that you would wait for the moment where he was going to hurt someone. And I didn't want to be like that. Because not all humans deserve it.

Just some.

And I think Elaine now falls into that category.

Everything about her drives me insane, thinking about it now, in my room, lying in bed, once again staring at the walls, the same old goddamn fucking walls. The same old emptiness, bringing itself in, making itself welcome while I wrestle with misery and lose two out of three falls. She's not a good person. She never was. I don't think she'll ever be. There's something in her that just doesn't make it RIGHT.

I want to block her out so I put my earbuds in and I turn up *Jane Doe* until I don't even hear the screaming, I just hear the drum beat and the guitar and then after a while, there's not even that, I fall into a land where it's nothing but pictures and I'm still the only one standing after Earth's biggest battle. The fault lines are no longer there. Cities and leaves and people are no longer here. I get lost in the perfect symmetry of a troubled unconsciousness until I suddenly remember something I shouldn't. I quick get up and step out into the hallway. No one else is awake. Mom doesn't even seem to be home. I go into their bedroom. I go into a secret hideaway in the floor that she doesn't even know about. I lift up the floorboard. And it sits there, waiting, laughing at me. And I lift it up, not heavy. It fits right into my palm, like it was meant to be there. And I start to sweat.

elaine

I didn't hear from her at all the following day. I didn't expect to. But I was waiting all day for another fight, and it never came, and I thought for a minute that hopefully the whole thing was over and done with. I didn't want to go through anything like that again. I had woke up with a pounding headache, my first hangover (not fun, never want to do that again), and the phone was ringing, and I thought it was her, but it turned out to be the boyfriend, who in the midst of all the bullshit last night, I totally had forgotten about. He called just to tell me to have a good morning and that he loved me again and I totally lost it on him about the previous night, about the graveyard and the drinking and how I wanted to learn more about death and he suddenly became very concerned for me. He said that he didn't want to hear me talking like that. He said he wanted to be with me for a very long time. We talked about our blowup a little bit more, tried to smooth out the details. But I had a feeling that he wasn't very happy with me still, even though I apologized a thousand times about talking about death. He got too sad. Sometimes he shuts down when it comes to those things. We promised to talk later and I wished him a good day and he said he loved me but I didn't say it back, and even though it made me happy before, today it just made me sad, like the words were useless, and it didn't feel the same. I wanted to go back to normal, but I don't think I could, because Bronwyn was sticking in my crawl more and more. I think that it's possible that she changed how I view the world. And I never wanted anyone to change that, but I'm getting the sickening feeling that it's way too late to go back now.

I had a long chat with Mom afterwards at the breakfast table. I told her about Bronwyn because before I didn't, since she was the type of person that

Mom would never want me to hang around. I omitted some details about our fight, and how I threatened to fight her, and just focused on the support group incident and the diner. I didn't want to get in about the graveyard. And she sat there for a long while in silence, sipping coffee, looking out the window. She was lost in a zone, contemplating if her daughter was starting to go down on a wrong path. I know that sounds dramatic, but that's how Mom thinks. After the locker room fight, she seemed ready to put me into some juvenile center or home school me. She thinks everything is the end of the world. I try telling her that Bronwyn meant well, and finally she set her coffee down and looked me in the eye, and told me not to associate myself with "people like her". And I tried asking her what she meant by that but she just shrugged it off and got herself ready for work. She kissed me on the head and told me she was glad I came to her if I was stressed and not to worry because I wasn't going to get involved with any people like Bronwyn anymore. She was going to talk to the church about letting me come back in, and before I could bring up what I was thinking about Dad and the voice and death, she was out the door, leaving me with her half-finished coffee, weak and watery and steaming.

I didn't get it out in time. I wanted to tell her how I felt, that I wasn't feeling suicidal, that I just wanted to know what she thought about a body once being here and now not being here and what the word meant to her. How she went to bed with that word. How she felt completely alone even though the product of her marriage sat right in front of her, young and pretty and inquisitive. But that was not to be today, I guess. I went up and got dressed and I went to work, like it was any other day. Maybe I was over thinking. Maybe it really was the vodka talking last night and not me. I made a solemn vow never to do that again or be around people who found drinking to be the answer to everything. It's stupid.

I got into the car and drove, no problems, no panics, just going and not worrying about anything. One of my favorite songs came on the radio, and I sang along with it, embracing the beauty of the day, and a life without such sadness and bullshit.

I sat down at my desk and someone had actually left me a Get Well card since I called out, and even though I hate it when people make a big deal out of nothing, it cheered me up and I carried it around with me all day in my back pocket.

One of my friends surprised me and came by on my lunch break and we went to my favorite place downtown, and although I wanted to tell her about what was going on, I kept it all inside, because I didn't want her thinking I needed to go see my therapist again, because nine chances out of ten that's what she would say if I told her about the sudden fascination on the insight of death. Bronwyn's name almost came up several times but it died on the tongue, and I'm surprised it even got that far, considering how much it makes me nauseous.

The rest of the work day was not that exciting. I tried several times to call the church and see if I could get back into support group and tell them all about what had happened with Bronwyn but every time I tried to call, someone needed something done and I had to hang up. I also tried to go online on the work computer and look up more about how people feel after death, like support groups for that as well, but I had a feeling someone would see it on the browsing history and I didn't need that linked back to me. So it would have to wait until I got home. I wasn't doing anything, anyway: the boyfriend was going to some game somewhere with his dad, and he knew I wouldn't enjoy it, so he never invited me. We texted back and forth throughout the day and although it felt a little strained, it seemed like he forgave me a little bit for what I said, and I knew that right then and there that my first priority was to patch up our relationship, because I knew he was the one for me. I didn't want to lose him. Scratch that. I couldn't lose him. He was too important. It made me feel love again, thinking about him.

But later on that night, all good feelings went away and the bad thoughts returned. I was thinking about crying to Dad, and Bronwyn trying to be nice and to clean up the headstone, and the cut on my arm. I had forgotten all about it. I hid it up without even thinking of it, but in the shower that night, I saw it, and all of it came back and punched me hard. It hurt to breathe for a while. I sat with the hot water beating down on my back and I clutched my hair just for something familiar to hold onto, but it wasn't helping. I felt sick. I remembered the phone call from the hospital - Mom, telling me Dad was dead. I remember seeing Bronwyn for the first time. Her black hair. Her ugly eyes. Her denial to believe that love was a real thing. I didn't get sick, but I held onto the sides, and I was there for a very long time, until my back was completely red from hot water stinging it, and finally I got out, and I tried to just forget it all, but we all know that forgetting is not the same as accepting. I tried to read a novel, but failed. I texted the boyfriend but he did not text back. So I went on Wikipedia about the fascination of death. I Googled everything I could about death. I wound up being awake until 4 AM, and all I got out of it was a horrible desire to see Dad, and not just a framed photo of him. I was tired of not knowing. I needed to move forward. I was scared and alone and I needed the old life back.

I called Bronwyn shortly before sunrise. And she would tell me.

bronwyn

There's a fine line between living your life alone and living it alone because you piss off everyone and no one wants to be around you. And Elaine is going to find out that difference real quick. She was foolish to turn down my well-meaning advice. I spent all day and all night deciding if I was going to do this. I didn't hear from her. Which was good. It came me plenty of time to hate and stew. And I finally came to the conclusion that I was just going to scare her. That's all I want to do. And then maybe she could be a new person without my fucking help, and she would be smart enough to leave me alone. She would be wise if she never came my way again. So I spent the day preparing on the best way to do it. I called off work. I listened to *O God The Aftermath* three times, getting in the right frame of mind. I put on one of my dad's favorite t-shirts, one of the few items I kept of his. Other than his fat face in my fucking dumb brain. And the other thing that I was going to give to Elaine to make sure she would remember this. So she would know what love and death and river and sky was all about. She thinks she has the upper hand. But she will soon find out that she never did. And it's a shame, because through all the pain and all the stories that I have in my life, contained and in control, this is the reckless one, bound for wreckage and a horrible ending and that's not what I wanted to have anymore. I wanted to go on the right road for a change. All I wanted to do was take pictures. But now, I would have to take someone's dignity, someone's reasoning. That doesn't seem moral.

But I'm fucking do it anyway.

Because that's what I need to do.

I wrote in my diary for a good portion of the afternoon. I would call her tomorrow to set up a time and a place. I will ask for her forgiveness and I will attempt to be friends with her one more time. If it does not work, then this is what will happen. It is the only ending, it is the only possible conclusion to what she has done. I cannot let her spread her anger to other people. So many people suffer with their parents gone, and she's making it so much worse than it has to be. My love, my way. My way was so much better, so much easier. It wasn't that bad. I wasn't going to ever hurt anybody with what I wanted to teach. I just wanted it to go smoothly, and she ruined the entire thing by being petty, by acting like she was queen of the war fields. She will lose and I will win and God willing, we will never hear from each other again. That would be the only thing that will make me happy. That ending, and a new beginning, and the only part that once again is terrible is the slow middle, the crawling bleeding middle, in which there is no escape and there is nothing that can stop it except time, and it makes me want to destroy everything, but I have to remember that I am better than that, I am always better than the middle, because the middle is what got Dad, and I will not fall victim to the same mistakes. Period. Amen.

I'm so much better than her.

I also uploaded a lot of pictures finally from my camera and I was arranging them into a binder that I had been neglecting for quite some time. Making the final details to the story in case something went very wrong. I didn't see it being that

242

way. But it was possible. My phone rang as I was arranging and I didn't see who it was. I answered anyway.

"Yes?"

"Bronwyn, why did you call off work?" It was Stan. Keyholder Stan. Trying to interrupt my art, my life. Motherfucker.

"I was too busy choking," I tell him.

"Choking?"

"Yeah, on your mom's chest hair," I say. "I'm done with your job, Stan. Find a new store associate to flirt with. You wouldn't last five seconds with me anyway," I say and I hang up the phone. I'm surprised I finally did that. It took me a long time to get the courage. But I couldn't see right anyway. I was blinded by stars and noise and whiskey and pictures of the world that I needed people to see. I would submit them someday, have an expo, have fancy drinks, and tell people that not only that I did this for a living, but I survived without a father, and I put Elaine Meadows in her place.

It was such an immature thing, to fixate and obsess over revenge, but that's how cities and worlds were built, with one emperor going after another, until the head was cut off, until the blood was drunk, until the flesh burned with all armies circling around screaming in unison. People fight with each other. That's a cornerstone of humanity. Without that, jaywalking, and voyeurism, where would America be? We'd be pansies. We'd be dirt. Our hearts would give up after only a few years and there would be no sense to fucking because we would die. I took a handful of my dad's t-shirt and I brought it to my nose and smelled. It didn't smell like him anymore. That went away a long time ago. But I wanted to get his attitude back in me. He would be proud of me this time. He wanted a tough daughter. He's getting one now. Hey Dad, we'll have a drink some day.

I laugh. A perfect lyric rolls into my head out of nowhere as I'm finishing organizing. I'll say it to Elaine when I see her dumb face soon enough. One of my all time favorites: "The world isn't against you, my dear, it just doesn't care." And it doesn't, which is the most beautiful part about that song, is that line. The realization that the pyramids and glass cages of greed and capitalism have no interest in your whiny bullshit, and I tried to teach you that, baby, but you've gone deaf and blind, and you have no way of talking yourself out of it.

It's a shame it went this way, friend.

I crawl into bed hours later attempting to convince myself to still go through with it. I had to, now. I prepared too much, I hate too much. I think of the way she hit me. I think of the things she said to me. She'll hurt someone someday. She's a monster. I don't like to say that about people, but she earned the title. I'll make a sign for her so she can wear it around her neck. I close my eyes. I don't want to read, I don't want to write, I don't want to drink. I suddenly yearn for the past. I think of kicking Dad. I think of how many ships I sunk. It's been a lot. There's a whole graveyard in that ocean somewhere. And it always moves. There's no one spot. Those souls will gang up on me soon enough. They have every right to. But I will go down kicking and screaming. If you don't do that, you're a fool.

I was close to an amazing dream until the phone rang. I was dreaming that I was normal and that I was on a swing set and it was raining and I had all the music in the world and none of it compared to anything else. But the old familiar shrill of technology woke me up. I fumbled for it and I held it up close. I was pissed. And I let it show. "WHAT?"

"Bronwyn."

My heart couldn't take it. "Elaine."

"Teach me about death."

I didn't know what to say to her honestly.

"I need to know. I want to see Dad again. I'm tired of...pretending that I think I know him when I really don't after all, and this life doesn't make sense without him. I'm not saying I want to die. I just...want to get a little closer. I don't know what I'm saying," and she started crying.

I had to do something otherwise I would be up all night talking in circles with her. And then I decided that I was going to be up all night anyway, regardless. I thought of my plan. I thought maybe this would be the right time, with no one around, with no one for her to run to, to scream and apologize to.

"Where do you want to meet?" I said.

"The graveyard," she said with no pause.

elaine

I sat leaning against Dad's headstone. I don't think he would have cared. It's my way now of showing I respect him. The old ways are gone. It's time to do new things. I had to come back out here. I can't avoid it forever. He has to see how I am. If he is watching from above, I don't think he's seeing the whole picture. I want him to see he can be proud of me. And I wasn't going to do him wrong. I waited quietly. She would be here soon, I hope.

I thought of everything I was going to say Bronwyn. I wanted her to know she has been a friend, even though it didn't seem like it. I just want her to believe that I'm not a bad person. I have all the faith in the world, and I need her to have some of it. I hope she doesn't feel bad about anything. I needed to apologize about the fight and the blood and her vodka. She needs to know I can be good. And my father does, too. He may have forgotten.

Finally I saw a car. And it was hers because I could hear the music all the way from the back of the graveyard. I guess we're not going for subtlety tonight.

She got out of the car wearing a long black coat and gloves and torn jeans. She left the headlights trained on us.

"Bronwyn, I'm sorry," I said.

"I don't give a fuck," she said and she pulled something out of her coat pocket. I couldn't see what it was right away but she stood there holding it in her hands like a present. I walked up to her and I peered through the blinding light.

And it was a gun.

I looked back, scared out of my mind. Her eyes never changed. She kept it out, like it was Communion, giving me the body of Christ. I didn't know what to do. My mouth went dry.

"Take it," she snarled.

I didn't.

"You want to know about fucking death, do it," she said. "It's my Dad's. It's a present. Go ahead, take it. Point it at yourself. Give yourself a little something."

"Bronwyn..."

"Listen, Elaine. You're fucked in the head. Like, totally. And you think you're so much better. You want to come out here and act like you're God? Fine. So be God, like I said. Take the gun. Go ahead. My dad only shot out of it once. It's cleaned and oiled. He showed me how. Did your dad teach you how to be God or only to be afraid of God?"

I didn't know what to say. "Bronwyn, listen," I started.

"What, Elaine? You ain't talking your way outta this. Take the gun. Do what you want to do with it. But I'm going to make something very fucking clear, and get this in your dumb little cunt head. You lay one more hand on me, you make one more threat, and your ass is going to be on the other end of this, and you can't run faster than what's in here."

"I'm trying to say I'm sorry!" I finally yelled at her. She wasn't getting it. This wasn't what this was all about. But she thinks it is. And I didn't know what else to do. I wanted her to put the gun away. My mouth couldn't make the words to say it. I knew that suddenly this was a big mistake. I had to leave. I tried to run around her but she stood in my way.

"You're not leaving until you take this," she said calmly.

"Fuck you, Bronwyn. Why are you doing this?"

"UH. WELL LET'S REVIEW. YOU CALLED ME OUT HERE. YOU WANTED TO KNOW WHAT I COULD GIVE YOU. YOU SAID TEACH. AND I'M TEACHING THE BEST WAY I KNOW FUCKING HOW."

"You're not going to hurt me, are you?"

"No. Jesus. I'm not going to hurt you. I have no interest in that. But just take it. It's yours. Go home. Take it home. Stare at it for a while."

"What is that going to do?"

"It'll help you, make you learn. It will become a new you. There's a lot of power in this thing. And it's not going to hurt you. Just take it. Please."

"Bronwyn."

"Elaine."

There was a silence, heavier than any other one I have ever known. Everything was swirling around in my head. I wanted to go home. I wish I never met her. I wish I would have just kept my mouth shut in church and believed in God and I wished I never questioned a goddamn thing because none of this would have ever happened. I just wished Dad never died. Because then I would be okay. I would be living a happy life.

"I wish my father never died," I said, tearing up. I was embarrassed but I was so beaten down and I had no other emotion left.

She watched me and she sounded like she was crying as well. "Me too, Elaine," she said.

"He was everything to me."

"I'm glad. Because he was nothing to me."

We watched each other in the dark, the old engine running, all the dead watching us, their new favorite show: us. They were never like us once in their life.

"Just let me go home."

"I can't let you do that. You can't go home."

"I don't want the gun."

"Yes you do."

But why? I couldn't talk. My throat hurt. There was no sense in taking something like that. It's a weapon. It's not meant to teach. She's insane. And I have to leave. I try to get around her again and she blocks the way. I'm losing my temper. I want to see my Mom. I want to call the police. I need to get away from the gun. I need to be a new person.

"Bronwyn," I say.

"I'm only giving you one more chance."

"I don't want your fucking chance."

"Elaine."

"I wish I never met you. I wish you would just die," I said. I meant it too. I felt God judging me, burning a hole right in me. I never said that to anyone before.

"I tried to help you," she said to me, holding the gun out to me.

"Get that fucking thing away from me."

And I didn't meant to slap it out of her hand but I guess she saw it coming and she kept a grip on it and we were fighting again. I was trying to get the thing out of her hand so she wouldn't show it to me anymore and she was trying to keep it and she kept saying Elaine, Elaine just stop just let go and we couldn't get in the right position to stop. The car lights did not give off good light and I tried to see her face, to tell her one more time that I just wanted to go back to my life and to forget about all this but for some reason I had to get it out of her hand. And she was battling me too and she wouldn't let go and she yelled ELAINE JUST LET GO and somehow something in my heart clicked and I knew something bad was finally coming.

And I knew I fucked up because I heard the gun go off. Towards me.

And Bronwyn screamed.

And breath left me.

And I fell and there was blood and pain.

And time kind of did this weird thing where it fucked itself over and paused and restarted again and words got really hard to form...........................

Noise.

And then and then and then and then shit. wait. shit. hold on. and after the bullet went in my throat and i couldn't breathe Bronwyn is asking me what I see what I see. i can't say it out loud so i'll think it but i see a sky a universe. she's pressing on my throat to hold the blood and i see the blood on her hands and i want it back in me and then and then and then i see a sky with men. i see men doing things i can understand and there's a river where kids are running to. i must say some of this out loud because now Dylan is kneeling over me with a phone to his ear and Bronwyn is repeating something back to me and i tell her not now there's a river love. there's this river and then hold and then there's men nearby and they're drinking the water like it's wine and i blood and blood and i shit i shit shit shit shit. and i try to hold on and Bronwyn is saying come on honey please, just hold, and i can't hold because there's a sky a river children. Dylan's holding my hand and now Bronwyn is holding the phone and they'r eblurry and there so blurr y blyyr. hold it baby hold it honey they're coming. and who's coming /\ who is there and she says they're coming to save you it's all my. it's all my. and i try to shake my head and there's something coming for my heart. it's the men. shit. and then. and then. a.nd. then. there's. a river, a sky. and they come together and they're drink in..g and their happy...jesus, jesus, stop. i must be dreaming i must be a dream. i must be this now. and i laugh and

Bronwyn is crying and Dylan Dylan poor Dylan is standing there holding my hand and jesus what a seen. what a terrible seen for a beautiful girl tomake. And I say to Bron}{wyn help Dylan please help him he's so sad and she's crying and she says Dylan who is Dylan Elaine there is no Dyla.n. And I can't talk. Dy.lan. Bronwyn. you know dlyan. He's my boyfriend and he says i'm so prettty. he wants me to marry me and bronyw-n says WHO and I s@y dyla!n and she says Elaine there is no one here but me no one no one at all and i'm like but he's my boyfriend and he said he loved he said he loved me me he loved. and bron,wyn is just watchin.g with ugly eye/s. and but Dylan why do you leave me now of all times but she screams Elaine: there is no one hear. But Mom said I was so prety. so, so...shit. and then. hold on. and Bronwyn's river flows into Dylan's hand and then i must bedreaming i mustbeadream. dad dad dad please let me go somewhere else i know i know please a river dad. i must be the most perfect dream my remaining blood will allow. Bronwyn says please don't oh but i must for you see...this is what we wait our whole life for

*